THE SIREN

M.R. Graham

THE SIREN

Copyright @ 2012-2015 MR Graham

http://quiestinliteris.com

COVER PHOTO BY

Greg Rakozy

https://unsplash.com/@grakozy

COVER DESIGN @ M.R. Graham

ISBN: 0692448179

ISBN-13: 978-0692448175

MORE BY M.R. GRAHAM

The Liminality Series

The Medium

The Mora

The Mage

The Martyr (Coming Soon)

In the Shadow of the Mountains

The Wailing

The Adventures of Morrigan Holmes

No Cage for a Crow

The Death of a Swan (Coming Soon)

The Van Helsing Legacy

We Shall Not Sleep

Poetry

Versos, or, The Things a Woman Learns on the Banks of the Great River

Papalotes: Songs of Texas

Also

The Truth of the Matter

Proof: A Short Tale of the Undead

Thank you, Davis, Nahrain, Dr. Montz, and Mr. Nimoy.
The stars are closer than ever.

CONTENTS:

AUGUST 12

Seattle area residents reported fireballs in the sky late Thursday night. The unusual display, which seems to have lasted several hours, consisted of bright white and blue meteor-like flashes of light that lit up the sky from Whidbey Island all the way to Tacoma.

According to eyewitness reports, the lights went streaking above the clouds along a north-south course that apparently followed the coast line. Carol Quinn, 48-year-old resident of Martha Lake, claims to have attempted to capture footage of the aerial lights, but has only a fried camcorder to show for her efforts. "It just caught fire as soon as I pointed it toward the sky," she told reporters during a telephone interview. She declines to submit the camcorder for inspection.

Astronomical expert Ian Gregsen, formerly employed by NASA and currently living in Lea Hill, says the pattern was consistent with space trash breaking up as it falls through the upper atmosphere. "I got chills," he said. "It was just like watching the Columbia happen all over again." In his professional opinion, the lights were most likely due to an old satellite breaking up as its orbit decayed. He cautions souvenir-seekers not to pick up any debris they might find, due to the risk of radiation.

ONE

There was a dead body on Sandie's back porch, and it was trying to get in.

She wrung the coffee out of the front of her shirt, made damn sure that all of her doors and windows were locked, and called Mike.

"Mike."

"Yeah? Sandie? That you?"

"You don't know anything about this, do you?"

"About what?"

"The zombie."

"Come again?"

"Mike, there's a zombie on my back porch. It's leaving smears on the glass door. Is it yours?"

"I... Could you repeat that?"

"Zombie, Mike. It's a dead body in a puddle of nasty, and it's leaving more nasty on my door. God, I can even smell it. This is one thorough job, man."

She edged away from the door, keeping an eye on the intruder beyond the glass. It was bloated and purple with decay, green and black fungus speckling its face. There was fluid coming out of its mouth and dripping from its nose. It had no eyes, and all indication of sex or age had rotted away.

"Robotic, maybe? One of its legs is about to fall off. You didn't sic one of your Cyber Derby friends on me, did you?"

There was a long moment of silence on the other end, then the sound of a slamming door and an engine revving.

"I don't know anything about it. But hey, are you going to be at home for a while? Can I come see it?"

"I sure as hell am not going out the back door. If it smells that bad inside... I'll put another pot of coffee on for you, okay? Come through the garage when you get here. Bring a shotgun or something just in case."

Sandie hung up and stuck her phone into the back pocket of her jeans, moving into the kitchen to refresh her cup. She went upstairs to change shirts, threw the stained one into the laundry, and washed her hands in the bathroom. The thumping and scratching from the back door was audible throughout the house, and it did not stop. She wondered whether she should be scared, but it all felt too much like a low-budget horror flick to be real.

A careful peek out of the hall revealed that the unwelcome guest was beginning to flag. The thumps were a bit further apart than they had been at first. Sandie cupped her hand over her nose and approached the door, with the reasoning that if it was going to get in, it would have gotten in already. The stink was nauseating.

"So," she said around her hand. "Are you here for my brains or what?"

The body clawed at the glass.

"You want a cup of coffee? Kudos on the makeup job, by the way, or whatever that is. It looks pro. Is that pig blood or something? You know you're going to be scrubbing my porch down later, right?"

The body hummed. It smacked a defleshed hand against the door, and the view distorted as the glass rippled with powerful bass vibrations.

Sandie fell back on her ass with a yelp, ruining another shirt with coffee.

"What the hell was that?" she demanded as the vibrations slowed and died. She picked herself up and crouched in front of the glass, staring into the creature's empty eye sockets. She received the unnerving impression that it was staring back. A dribble of black spilled from its mouth and splattered on the cement outside. There was half a grasshopper in it.

"Oh," Sandie said. "You're real, aren't you? Oh, God, you're real." That panic started to well up, along with the bagel she had eaten for breakfast. "Oh, God, oh my God."

She reached back and pulled the phone from her pocket, hit redial as fast as she could. Mike's phone began to ring. The body outside stared through the glass, its swollen tongue hanging down to its chin. It slumped sideways, pressing its shoulder against the glass.

Sandie gasped into the receiver, and there was a click.

"Sandie? You okay?"

"Right. No. Cops. Hurry."

"Wh-?"

She hung up and punched in 9-1-1.

The body hummed. It resonated, a clear, bell-like tone. Dust sifted down from the ceiling. The glass warped and undulated like a sheet of water, then burst inward with a pop. Sparkling fragments rained down amid a shockwave of sound.

The phone beeped, sparked and died, and Sandie was on her knees, feeling oddly mellow in the moments before she passed out.

TWO

In the dream, Sandie was weightless. She had dreamed that sort of thing before, though, and understood that it would not last. When she dreamed that she was floating, it was only a matter of time before she dreamed that she fell.

It was an odd sensation, floating there in the dream. She could hear the world – cars and a dog and the rumble of a jet passing overhead – but there was nothing to see. She tried to raise her hand in front of her face, but she had no hand, either.

I'm a Presence, she decided. *A Presence floating in space.* That was comforting, because a Presence could not fall. She listened to the sound of the highway.

damaged?

It was not so much a voice as a thought, less of a word

than an impulse, sort of like Sandie imagined binary code might feel to a computer. She tried to shake her head, figure out whether it was her ears or her brain that had received the message. But she had no ears, and it did not feel like she had a brain, either, and as she thought about it, she became more and more certain that she had not heard anything but an idea... whatever that meant.

sorry did not intend will attempt help. listen? tiny mind inside tiny head so quiet in here much feeling. come back now if able some difficulty will try compensate. stand by.

Then she was moving. It was not very fast, and a sense of extreme effort from somewhere nearby struck her as amazingly inefficient, but she was moving, and the sound of the highway was fading. There was a quiet scraping and squishing, like something gelatinous being dragged over rocks.

I think I'm inside the zombie.

?

Never mind. God, what if it ate me? Am I zombie guts? This had better frigging not be Purgatory, or I am never spending money on a scapular ever again...

explain?

Nothing, sorry. I guess internal monologue is sort of hard to censor. So are you my like my shoulder angel or something?

don't know maybe.

That's not helpful.

The other presence radiated perplexity but did not have a better answer. The slow dragging continued. Then there was a thump.

Another thump, and violent swearing, and then the world was tangible again, and Mike was hoisting her onto the couch. He smelled like apple cider, but there was also the smell of burnt electronics and liquefied flesh, and the last of those was probably the best explanation for the squeezing sensation around Sandie's stomach. Her shirt was wet, and the ceiling was white, and nothing else made very much sense.

"Sandie. Damn, come on, girl. Come on, baby," – he patted her cheek – "That's it, eyes open. No, don't throw up. How many fingers?"

"Piss off."

"Close enough. Don't move, there's an ambulance coming. What did he hit you with?"

"E minor, I think."

"I don't get it."

"Me neither."

Mike got her a glass of water. She asked for coffee, but he firmly refused. There were cops and paramedics, and no one was particularly impressed. There were a few handprints, but they were gooey and yielded no clues. There were a few bruises, but nothing that could have knocked someone out. There was nothing missing, either, so they could rule out insurance fraud. Sandie received reassurance and a sheet of heavy plastic to tape over the broken window. Mike got a bucket and a brush and went to work on the back porch while a can of soup reconstituted on the stove.

"So you think it was real, huh?"

Sandie popped open a root beer with a shrug. "That's what I saw. It was amazing, Mike. I mean, this thing just shattered the window like an opera singer with a wine glass. And it was dead. Like seriously dead. Like I've seen hamburgers more lively than this thing, and it wanted in."

Mike did not need words to express his skepticism. It came through just fine in the way his scrubbing brush paused between strokes.

"No, I know. I know I'm traumatized or something, and it's probably all in my head, but they asked me what I remembered, and that's what I remember. Anyway, I called you before I passed out, so everybody knows that there was something there, whether it was a prank or whatever."

"Must have been a good one. I sure wish I got here before the bastard got away. I could have beat him up for you. How come you didn't? Beat him up, I mean. You're tough, you could have kicked his face in or something."

"Maybe he gassed me or something. Or had a friend

already in the house. Anyway, I remember the glass breaking, and that's it. I must have been out before he even got inside."

"He didn't get inside, unless he put plastic down first. There's none of this crap on your carpet."

"At least there's that. I didn't really want to have it steamed."

Mike dropped the brush into the bucket and grimaced at his hands; his fingernails were crusted with grime. Sandie got the door for him and led the way back inside.

"You didn't have to do that," she said. "I would have gotten to it eventually."

"By which you mean you would have let the neighborhood raccoons deal with it."

"Pretty much."

Mike sighed and made as if to brush his hair out of his eyes, remembering at the last moment that he was dramatically unclean. He made for the kitchen instead and shouted over the tap.

"You should come stay with me tonight. You can call a glazier tomorrow, but you shouldn't be staying here with that hole sitting there. Anyone could just walk in."

"Yeah, and then one of your old ladies sees me leaving, and the whole parish flips out. I'll get myself a hotel room, or something."

"Forgive me, I forgot about your collar fetish." He winked as he rolled his sleeves back down. "But seriously, I think you should have someone with you. Moral support, y'know."

"Nah, I'm tough. If the place has a coffee maker and cable, I'll be fine. Might have to call in sick tomorrow, though. Man, Mike, you should have seen that thing. If I'd gotten pictures, I'd be all over the news. It was tabloid-worthy."

She sank into a chair and pulled her knees up to her chest, balancing her can of root beer between her bare feet. The pressure on her stomach was lightening, and the morning's bagel seemed very far away.

"If you've got time," she said, "I sort of feel like going out for lunch."

They split a fajita plate at Tia Gloria's Chinexican Grill. Mike went back to the rectory, and Sandie bunked up with an overnight bag at a cheap motel. A boyfriend would be good, she thought – one who was not a priest. A five-dollar bottle of wine would be even better. She hiked across the street to the convenience store and picked up a six-pack instead, then hiked back and flicked on a documentary about real-life encounters with angels. It was saccharine and ridiculous, and that was just what she needed.

Connie called just as the pasty woman with breast enhancements was recounting her near-death experience with a dark highway and an unexpected cow.

"*Mama*," she said with a pop of her gum. "Girl, where you at? I'm gonna take you to get your nails done. Like hell I'm gonna let you sit there and get all freaky about this."

Sandie sighed and crunched the phone between her shoulder and her ear as she slipped her blue jeans back on. Girl talk was the last thing she wanted, but she had to admit that her nails were looking pretty crappy. She gave the address and put her third can of beer back in the fridge. She clicked the television back off, but the people in the next room must have had the volume turned way up, because she could have sworn she heard a word through the wall.

gone?

THREE

It was only reluctantly that Sandie went to work on Friday morning, but she had to admit that her nails looked awesome. She had settled on neon blue, and Connie had loaned her an eye shadow to match. It gave her a tiny bit of extra confidence, just enough to face a steady stream of coffee-hungry commuters. She flitted between the espresso machine and the rows of syrup bottles, filling orders while she deflected curious sympathy from her co-workers.

Connie was the worst.

"So, he didn't take anything?" she verified for the twentieth time. She popped her gum and flipped her glossy black mohawk to the other side of her head.

"Nope. At least, I haven't noticed anything missing yet."

"Nothing?" Connie asked again. She leered and winked. "Nothing at all? I mean, you don't think he snuck in and ravished your unconscious body?"

"What the hell? Where do you get this stuff?"

"From Padre. Not that last part, I mean. He just told me you had a break-in. Bo-ring. Doesn't make a good story to say some guy broke in and then just ran off."

"Yeah, well, said guy didn't have a whole lot of equipment, if you know what I mean. Might not even have been a guy. I couldn't tell."

"Ooh, that's cool. I could dig that. I mean, not the felon part, but androgynous is hot."

"Connie, please shut up."

Sandie handed over a mocha latte, extra foam, to a customer who left more quickly than they usually did. No tip.

Connie leaned against the counter and adjusted her nose ring with an expression of intense concentration. She had chosen dark brown at the manicure session the day before, and her lips and eyelids were the same color.

"Come on, *mama*," she said. "You were swearing up and down yesterday that you wouldn't even come in today, but here you are. What gives? I'm gonna bug you until you tell me, and you know it."

Brandon stuck his head out of the back and adjusted his managerial pin with a self-important air. "Look," he said, "would you two just go on break already? You're grossing out the patrons. Not to mention me."

Indeed, there was a banker by the trash can, trying desperately to get his muffin out of its wrapper so he could leave, and two nuns by the window with their faces purple. A harried-looking woman wearing sneakers and pearls had curled her lip up so far, it was in danger of disappearing into her nose. Only the guy with dreadlocks and a hennaed face looked vaguely amused.

"I'm traumatized," Sandie protested. "Doesn't that come with some venting privileges?"

"Not when you're venting on open comestibles."

"Ew. Point taken."

But the sensation of being watched did not diminish as Sandie shuffled into the back to hang her apron from its peg and washed the last of the flavored syrup from her hands. She looked around and saw Connie tapping a cigarette into her hand with intense concentration, and no one else present. Brandon had gone up to man the counter during the mid-morning lull.

"God, this thing has me so frigging paranoid..." She slapped on another coat of lipstick and refreshed her smudged eyeliner.

"What, you think this guy's following you?"

"I don't know. I doubt it. But look, you can't go telling anyone about this, okay? I went downstairs yesterday and there was this zombie – dead body – on my back porch. I thought it was some asshole pranking me, you know? So I called Mike, because you know he's got those friends from college. But then it breaks the window in and knocks me out, and now every time I close my eyes, there's this voice..."

"Excuse me? And you haven't been to the hospital yet because...?"

"Because I'm not hurt. I think I'm just freaked out, but my stupid Freudian subconscious isn't doing anything to help that."

"You're hearing voices. That's not a good thing, *mama*. Come on. Now you're freaking me out, and I gotta smoke." Connie picked up her purse and a bottle of water out of the employee's fridge and went out back into the alley.

Sandie followed, but the alley looked like an ideal place for a zombie attack. She hung back in the doorway while Connie lit up.

"Not voices. Just one voice, and it's more like I'm dreaming it. It was all last night, and then it woke me up, so I watched some TV, and then it was again when I went back to sleep. First it was trying to find me, and then it got distracted by something and like wandered off."

"Do you think it's... you know?"

"It's what?"

Connie flicked the accumulating ash from the end of her cigarette and ran her tongue across her teeth. Her tongue-ring made a clicking noise as it passed over her incisors.

"You know. Part of your thing. Maybe you're picking up something extra."

"I'm good at reading faces, that's all. If I'm reading minds now, I need a psych ward more than I need an MRI. If I'm reading a zombie's mind..."

"So you do think it was a zombie."

Sandie shrugged. "Mike asked me the same thing. I don't really know. That's what it looked like, but I can't really believe it. I mean, I think I did. For a moment. It freaked me the hell out, but now, in the light of day..."

A car alarm went off at the end of the alley. Underneath the sound of traffic from the Anderson Loop, there was a whisper.

hungry...

"Crap."

"What?"

"Nothing. I'm going back in, now."

gone where? coming now.

FOUR

Mike brought a pizza for lunch, and the crew piled into the back of his minivan to enjoy it. He disconnected the battery to keep the interior lights from eating up the juice and opened all of the doors to invite a breeze. Even so, the sun turned his car into an oven. At least the pizza was hot.

The sign on the Baptist church down the street flashed: "Pray for Rain."

"You feeling okay?" Mike asked. He had on a red plaid shirt that almost managed to hide the pizza-sauce stains. His collar was curled up in the cup holder in the front seat.

"Better," Sandie said. She bit off a string of cheese and helped herself to an orange soda from the cooler. "I mean, it's hard to stay freaked out when you're working the morning rush and you've got twelve caffeine addicts yelling at you over the counter. Would have been easier if Connie would stop bugging me, though."

Connie offered an angelic smile from her place on the bumper. "Not my fault you're loca, *mama*."

"I guess you guys don't listen to news radio in there, do you?"

"Not often. Brandon says politics is bad for business. Why?"

"Old lady in Castle Hills was out walking her dog this morning and found a body. She said it made a humming noise - said it was like a microwave - and then it crawled away."

"I told you! I so totally told you!"

"Yeah, so anyway, the cops are looking for the guy, now. They're afraid he's a leper or something contagious. Some flesh-rotting disease."

"Ew. Okay, I'm glad I let you scrub my porch down for me."

Mike wrinkled his nose and squinted up one eye. "I want you to go to the hospital. Just to make sure, you know? I went in to get some blood tests as soon as I heard. They said that was a damn good idea, so I want you to do the same."

"Now?"

"Soon."

hungry.

"Oh, screw it. Fine, I'll go. Can you cover for me, Connie?"

=

The emergency room was full of the machine-gun cadence of Spanish arguments - arguments with staff, with spouses, with uncooperative children, with other patients who may or may not have been waiting longer. Underneath the surge of conflict, there was an occasional cough, a whimper. And underneath the sound of sickness, there was a paradoxical stillness, the hush of fear.

Sandie pulled her little notepad out of her purse and flipped to a clean page.

Black is not the color of death, she wrote.

It's white.
White walls
White floors
White jackets
White faces
White sheets.
It's sharp and acrid
a white smell
burning and blinding
condensing into white pills.

She put the notebook away and let her eyes drift out

of focus on the television set hanging from the ceiling by the window.

"Melindrez, Sandra?"

A very pleasant, very old woman listened patiently while Sandie explained her concerns. No, there was no direct contact with it. No, I didn't touch the fluids. Yes, it smelled like rotting meat. And by the way, is it normal to hear voices?

"You've just been through a harrowing experience, honey," the nurse said as she packaged up an ampoule of blood. "Most people feel a bit odd after something like that. I wouldn't get worried unless it gets worse or keeps up for more than a week or two. Of course, if you want to talk to someone, I can make you a list of some good counselors..."

Sandie ended up with a list of some good counselors and a promise that she would get the results of her blood work soon.

"And I really wouldn't worry about it too much," the nurse said. "I heard that report on the news, and I can tell you right now that poor person isn't a leper. Not sure what, of course, but if you didn't touch, you're almost definitely fine."

Sandie bought herself a doughnut and a bottle of apple juice from the hospital cafeteria and consumed them thoughtfully on her way out to her car.

Dissociation, she decided. *They're my own thoughts, but my id or whatever can't recognize them as such, because I'm in shock and under stress and stuff.* She dropped the list of counselors into the passenger seat under her purse. She could afford to give it a couple of days, see whether the problem would fix itself. An ER visit by itself put enough of a dent in her rainy day fund without the added expense of a therapist's chair.

She went back to the motel and showered thoroughly to rid herself of the lingering smell of disinfectant, took two doses of cough syrup to kill any budding dreams, and crawled in bed.

It was waiting for her.

hungry. attempt repair fail too much calculate under memory damage.

There was a dizzy quality to the thought, something that Sandie found familiar. It was very similar to that feeling from earlier, woozy and slightly nauseated after watching part of herself drained into a clear tube.

help.

What do you want? You can't have my brain.

help. tiny animals tiny minds too quiet too quiet too quiet. outside don't hear. only you hear.

But the word had very little to do with ears. It meant knowing, sensing, understanding, together-being.

But what do you want? And why me?

hungry.

Then something shifted. Outside their little bubble of communication, there was fear. Sandie could hear lights flashing, red and blue, and a pair of snakeskin boots. Disgust, then reluctant pity. There were words, but they were garbled beyond understanding. And It soaked them up, the fear, revulsion, and compassion – soaked them up eagerly like a vacuum.

All around, there was a hum, deep, curious, and penetrating. It shook Sandie to the bone, and it brought a flood of information. Blueprints. Frequencies. Like sonar.

Sandie woke up when her hip hit the floor.

"This isn't real," she said aloud while she unwound herself from the scratchy motel sheets. "It's not real. I'm not nuts. It'll go away in a few days."

She pressed the heels of her hands into her eyes and leaned against the side table, focusing on the labored huff of the air conditioner and the cigarette smell of the ancient carpet.

hungry.

She could feel it, too. She could know/sense/understand/hear it, a vague emptiness that it would take more than a hamburger to fill. She could feel it like it was real. A nervous lump rose in her throat.

"Oh, God, I don't want to lose my mind..."

The anxiety siphoned away down that incomprehensible uplink, drained away and filled a small portion of the void.

more...

FIVE

All Sandie learned from her very expensive blood tests was that there was no reason for her to have paid for very expensive blood tests. She did not have leprosy, or hepatitis, or any of a number of different anemias. The news was a comfort, but the check was not.

Sandie bought a book of stamps and sent a stack of poems away to the offices of *Lead Soldiers*, thinking that a small royalty would at least begin to fill the dent that a new door and a medical bill had left in her bank account.

"Maybe you could take up a special collection for me," she told Mike as she got him a glass of water – root beer was an unnecessary expense.

"Meh," he said. "Charitable though the cause may be, it doesn't really work that way."

"Shame. I'm going to start getting really sick of ramen

in a week or two."

"You can always come share with me. For some reason, people are always bringing me leftover barbecue. Which is nice, don't get me wrong. But they must think I eat like a football team or something. I mean, a gallon of potato salad? Really?"

Sandie was silent. She picked at a moth hole in her tee shirt and crossed her legs, first one way and then the other, and said nothing.

Mike sat forward and put on his Confession face, the one that said he was ready to listen and would not, under any circumstances, laugh.

"What's the matter? You don't like potato salad?"

"There's a voice haunting me."

A car alarm went off, and the dogs next door set up an answering ruckus. Outside, someone started shouting for the world to just shut up.

"It's worse when I'm asleep or really tired, but it's gotten to where it's all the time, now. It started right after the break-in. And it's not really a voice, more like thoughts. Like tuning in to someone's mind. Sometimes it's aimed at me, like its talking to me, but most of the time it's just thinking about whatever, trying to figure things out. It's looking for something, but I don't think it knows what. It scares the hell out of me, but then it... like... I don't know. Like it sucks the fear out of me. Like it needs that. Does that make sense?"

Mike shut his eyes and opened them again very slowly. He set his glass of water on the end table, chewed his lip, laced his fingers, and took a preparatory breath.

"Have you considered seeing someone about this?" The light filtered blue through the sheet of plastic that sealed the door and fell across his face – his Last Rites face.

"Yeah, but I'm broke. Plus, I'm not convinced that I'm crazy. I mean, it's looking pretty likely that I am, I admit, but I'm not actually that stressed, and the paramedics said I didn't hit my head that hard, and it just seems like one hell of a coincidence."

"You mean that you get attacked by a dead body, and now you're hearing voices, and you think that they're both real, and related."

"Yeah, pretty much. I like that better than the idea that I'm schizo. Only..."

"What?"

"You don't think I'm possessed or anything, do you?"

There was a pause, long enough to make Sandie uncomfortable.

"At this point, I really couldn't say." He sat back again and folded his arms with a look of healthy skepticism, blue eyes narrowed in thought. "You know we have to rule out insanity before even looking into that. But if you're worried about it, frankly, that can't be doing your mental state any good."

"Mike. Father... There is someone else in my head. Being worried about it is pretty natural, I'd say. And if it's... gonna start getting worse, or... taking me over or something... Crap, I mean..."

Mike got up and crossed over to the couch, grabbing the tissue box in passing. He set the box on Sandie's knees and draped his arm across her shoulders, wincing as she jammed her head up under his chin.

"Baby," he said, "you are the toughest girl I know. If anyone has the guts to handle weirdness, it's you."

=

It was moving again as soon as Sandie got into bed. Slow, labored, starving, and determined. It dragged itself blind through suburbia to the sound of sprinklers until a late-night bicyclist hit a bump and went sprawling. There was blood and garbled plosives that were probably cursing. There was anger. Footsteps. More cursing. Then silence and horror.

damage. breach outer boundary understand easy repair. little effort. results inconsequential stimulus unknown cannot replicate. unsatisfactory. insufficient.

It absorbed the anger and the horror and moved on, leaving the cyclist behind, but it was not enough.

It found the freeway and followed a stream of

frustration around the Loop, noisy and congested even in the wee hours. Dotted between the horns and brakes were flashes of road rage.

unsatisfactory. insufficient. inefficient. spontaneous unpredictable cannot be harnessed.

What are you looking for?

need... will recognize object when located.

What if you don't find it? And what do you need me for?

unknown. anticipate negative consequence. contact is a preventative measure.

Preventative of what?

isolation.

It stopped thinking, then, and started listening hard. There was a sensation like stretching out, and Sandie found a familiar pattern. It was distorted by Someone Else's perception, filtering through a mind that had no idea what to make of it, but Sandie recognized a jazz band. The bass line pounded through her id with fierce abandon, and the entire universe resonated wildly to the frenetic strains of improv.

It hummed an answering harmony, stretching out even further to touch a whirl of elation. Wrapped up tight in the voice of a twelve-string, people were dancing, shouting, and radiating more feeling than Sandie could take in. They never missed a few stolen laughs, a couple of missed beats as It sucked everything in, soaked up droplets of joy like a vast metaphysical sponge. It was moving again, pressing closer, right up against the vibrating walls, and the movement was easier, more natural, and the vibration was in its hands as they knitted together, condensed into something whole, and there was a body, a connection, a solidity, and then eyes opened and saw bricks painted green, the outside of the bar...

=

The adrenaline rush jarred Sandie awake, and she sat up in bed with a grunt, one hand pressed to her hammering head.

"Holy crap."

Instinctively, she reached for her cell phone on the night stand, eyes passing over the digital clock. Quarter to midnight. Mike would still be up. There was nothing to tell him, though – at least, nothing she could explain. She set the phone back down and rolled onto her side, settling back onto the pillow. There was plenty of night left to find out what would happen next, get an idea of what was going on, like an addictive serial publication.

But when she closed her eyes, there was no one there.

SIX

The rest of the night was quiet, and so was Sandie's morning. If the alarm went off, she never heard it, and she slept hard until nearly ten, when her phone rang.

"I think it's gone," she told Connie. "I mean, I don't want to jinx anything with optimism, but at least it's gone on vacation."

She drank her coffee black and supervised the installation of a new door. She picked up the phone to call Mike, but remembered belatedly that he had a noon Mass, and set it down again to wait until later.

Local news entertained her until the thump came from the new door.

A person's silhouette was visible through the frosted glass, standing still and dark beneath the shade of the back porch.

The thump came again – not a knock, but a meaty thwack as though the visitor was trying to come straight through. Then there was the horrible squeak of skin sliding down the glass.

Sandie's lip curled. She added Windex to her mental grocery list and stood up, grabbing a heavy wooden candle stick from the end table as she went to answer the door. *Tomorrow*, she thought, *I'm going gun shopping.*

The silhouette ran itself against the door again, like a drunk who had lost the concept of solid matter. No one ever came to the back door any more, not since Doña Elvira from the house across the creek had died. Delivery men never came to the back door. Cable men never came to the back door. Since Doña Elvira, only dead bodies came to the back door.

Sandie turned the knob and peered outside.

A most peculiar individual peered back. It was naked and bizarrely generic, archetypal, the sort of thing that one might envision if one's only knowledge of humanity came from the first paragraph of an encyclopedia entry. It cocked its bald head and studied the mud mat on the ground with flat, black eyes, its slender, hairless arms encircling its slender, hairless chest. Though Sandie stared in consternation, there was nothing of interest between its slender, hairless legs. And though its eyes were fixed on the cement, somehow she knew that the thing itself was watching her closely. Waiting.

Slowly, as though uncertain of its own body, the creature reached out one pallid hand...

Sandie slammed the door. It failed to catch. She grabbed hold of the wriggling fingers, shoved them back outside, and slammed the door again, threw the bolt, fastened the chain, and raced upstairs to hide in the closet.

"I'm not messing with this," she muttered to her knees in the mothball-scented darkness. "I am so not messing with this right now. Nope. No frigging way. Can't make me. I refuse to let this be real."

From the bottom of the closet, surrounded by wool and denim, there was no way a thumping creature could reach her. She listened hard, but if it was still there, she could not hear it. The pipes creaked, and the air conditioner rumbled, and her breath stirred the fringe on an old poncho, but downstairs was as far away as another planet. She leaned back against the wall and watched the slash of light that filtered beneath the door. Nothing came for her.

Five minutes passed, then fifteen, and Sandie took a deep breath and admitted that she was being stupid. She crawled out of the closet and sat very still in the afternoon sunlight that pooled on the carpet, listening. Still, there was nothing. It was probably gone.

She was not even scared, Sandie realized, just overwhelmed and pissed off and very much unamused at

37

the persistent stupidity of life in general. She picked up her candlestick and took it back downstairs.

The silhouette was still there, standing inhumanly still just beyond the frosted glass. Still waiting.

"I - DON'T - NEED THIS," Sandie shrieked at the door. Then she went about ignoring it.

She did three loads of laundry, including the coffee-stained shirts she had been soaking in detergent. She cooked a box of macaroni and ate it with a sliced hotdog wiener. She turned up the air conditioner and checked local news for a weather report. It was over a hundred degrees outside. A twinge of guilt made her glance at the door, but she told herself that the thing could use the garden hose if it really needed to. Or it could just go away and hang out wherever it belonged. She ran the dishwasher and sat in front of her laptop for half an hour, trying and failing to produce a good poem.

It never moved once.

She showed up unexpectedly at the Joe Haus and worked a four hour shift under Brandon's skeptical eye, logging inventory because business was slow.

"I need some no-thinking time," she said when he asked her what the hell she thought she was doing. "I didn't punch in, don't worry."

He told her to go ahead and punch in anyway. "Just... call ahead or something," he said with a bewildered frown.

When she got home, it was too dark to see anything on the back porch. She turned on the outside light and sighed at the shadow that fell across the floor.

"God, you must be some kind of idiot," she said softly, not really knowing whether she was talking to it or to herself. She opened the door half an inch, using her foot to keep it from opening any further.

The thing was still there, still naked, still weird. It had gone from staring at the mud mat to standing with its eyes unfocused, as though it was listening. The eyes were all pupil, veinless white and inky black with no trace of color in between. A tiny pink gecko had stuck itself to the creature's cheek. There was nothing frightening about a gecko.

Sandie opened the door a little bit wider. The gecko fled, more scared of her than it was of the oddity it had chosen for its perch.

I can do this, Sandie thought. *It's not doing anything, anyway*.

"Do you need something?" she asked aloud.

The eyes did not move, but Sandie could feel Its attention gathering on her, and a barely perceptible vibration shivered in her bones for a fraction of a second.

"Holy crap," she said. "It's you, isn't it?" She was torn between being pissed that It was back and being relieved that she would not have to deal with something new.

?

The thought was faint and weak.

repaired. attempt. too costly. lost source.

It was so tired, so empty that Sandie wanted to cry, but It sucked that out of her and left her with only the dregs of compassion.

more? There was no hope in the question.

"I'll see what I can do." She took It by the arm – Its flesh was cold and stiff – and brought It inside.

SEVEN

The thing sat still and silent on Sandie's couch, swathed in the oversized black shirt and faded jeans of some long-ago boyfriend. Its white hands rested, motionless, on Its denim-clad thighs while Its expressionless eyes stared through the wall into nothing. It had not moved in more than half an hour, not even to breathe - which only made sense, Sandie thought, since It had been dead and rotting the last time she had seen It.

On the other hand, it was hard to be sure that this visitor was the same one that had shattered her window. The faces were so different, and this one was not dripping, but the voice in her head was the same. It felt the same, what few flashes she had gotten from It.

But after a few minutes, It seemed to have given in to exhaustion and fell into quiet muttering that filled the back of Sandie's head.

She tried to help. She dug up old clothes and helped It to dress, a process not dissimilar to trying to clothe a rag doll. She asked what It needed, both aloud and silently, mind-to-mind, but It was sick and weak and could not answer.

I'm developing a habit, she thought as she called Mike.

"I'm not really sure how to explain," she said in response to the worried voice on the other end. She gave the thing on her couch a skeptical glance. It still had not moved. "I just think you should come see this. I need... a second opinion, I guess."

"Come see what?"

"Just come, please?"

Mike grabbed his keys and hung up.

Sandie sat down again. There was a heavy wooden candlestick on the floor beside her chair, but it had been fifteen minutes since she had looked at it and longer still since she had reached for it. The only potential threat in the room may as well have been a statue, for all the threatening It did.

Its eyes did not move, but Sandie could feel It considering her. Quiet. Speculative. She shifted uncomfortably. It wanted something; that was obvious, but It seemed to have chosen to make her guess.

"Look," she told the side of Its head, "I don't know

why you came to me, but I'll do what I can. I mean, within limits, you know? But I'm going to have to know what you want before I can give it to you. I'll try, don't get me wrong. I just need to know what you want."

The body sagged, slumping sideways against the arm of the couch while the mind inside curled in on Itself. They were separate, Sandie realized; the body was only a vehicle for Whatever was driving it. Keeping muscles locked, a torso sitting upright, eyes open – it took too much effort.

She half-stood and touched the cold, white cheek. Dead. Sandie snatched her hand back and tucked it up against her ribs, trying to get rid of the disgusted tingle in her fingertips. There was a dead body sitting on her couch.

Something flickered behind her eyes, and Sandie jumped. It was like a memory, but hard to translate, couched as it was in a framework of frequency and tone and amplitude.

a dying rumble shivers through her core, shaking her on the deepest level imaginable. it disrupts. there is high frequency – bright – and low frequency – dark.

Sandie blinked. Reality was still there. The couch, the body, the new door, and the sheet of blue plastic folded neatly in the corner, all were plainly visible. But there was more than that.

she hears rock, air, intense heat, and something shrill,

43

something wrong. it beats against her and makes holes, skips in the beat. dissonance. she runs from it, but it is not really running; she floats, compresses, snatching at the air and pulling herself away.

It faltered for a moment. The Thing inside the body was resting. Sandie could sympathize; it was a bad memory. She squeezed her eyes shut and tried to figure out what she was seeing. Feeling. Whatever it was. She thought she should have been a lot more alarmed than she was.

It stirred again.

she wanders, alone. there is complete silence. the sensation is unpleasant. the silence is unfamiliar; perhaps the silence has not always been, but she cannot remember a time when it was not. somewhere, there are others. on the edge of consciousness, there are sparks, low notes, vibrating. they are unfamiliar. they do not touch, do not mesh, do not synchronize, do not harmonize. dissonance.

they are confined. small bodies, small minds, trapped inside small bodies. physical. material. they clash with one another. they feel, but they cannot feel her. they clash, resonate, vibrate in conflict with one another. they touch. little animals, flesh and blood.

she finds one, circles the mind like a moth around a candle flame. like a candle flame, the mind is small and bright. she is dim. soft and vast. unconfined. the little animal does not even know she is there. disconnect.

skip.

there are many attempts. no communication. failure.

skip.

a discarded shell. empty, no mind inside. just a shell, untended, decaying, abandoned. she borrows it, but only with reluctance. it is badly damaged, and she has no template, no way to repair it to normal specifications. it is time for research. scan. resonate. she searches for the average, the norm, compiling a composite understanding of hundreds of specimens. there is one mind in the distance, bright but broader, capable, compatible. maybe there is no need for this expenditure – it is costly, too expensive, and there is too little reserve, not enough energy to repair the vehicle. it is preferable to attempt communication with the anomaly.

"You mean me," Sandie said aloud. "I'm the anomaly." She could feel herself in the memory.

"So, are you here for my brains, or what?"

failure to communicate.

Her head hurt, somewhere deep inside her skull. The body on her couch did not move. She checked her watch, but it was still far too early to expect Mike, as much as she would have liked some moral support.

"Failure to communicate, my ass. You broke into my frigging house. I thought you were going to kill me or something." She wanted to be angry, but It was still pulling greedily at that corner of her mind, and the most she could manage was pragmatism.

failure to communicate. template formation successful.
repaired...

The thud and whirl of a jazz band pounded for a moment in Sandie's head, and she gripped the arm of the chair hard to keep herself from falling. It was the sound of elation and sustenance.

"You eat feelings. You ate their feelings and... de-rotted? So why did you come back here?"

discontinued. you hear. you will help.

"You mean the bar closed. The people went home..." She had said that she would help, and she regretted it. She pushed her hair back into a ponytail and fished a rubber band out of her pocket to secure it.

"I know a bluegrass bar that might be open. I'll drive you, you do your do, and then you go away. I don't know what to do with you."

=

Mike arrived to find Sandie struggling to stuff a dead body into the backseat of her car.

"We're going clubbing," she said.

"Oh, Christ," Mike said, and he meant it.

EIGHT

There was a dead body in the back seat, and it was staring at Mike.

"It's not staring at you," Sandie told him. "Actually, I'm not sure that it can see."

"It?"

"Well, it's not a he or a she. I... didn't exactly check, but it was kind of hard not to notice..."

"I don't think I needed to know that."

And still it stared.

Mike kept a firm hold on Sandie's hand until they got on the Loop and she needed both hands to drive. She looked grim and determined in the green glow of the dashboard lights. It talked to her, she said, talked to her in dreams the way angels were said to do sometimes. Whatever was riding in that weird, hairless body, it was no angel. He watched Sandie's face carefully, keeping tabs on the thing in the back seat from the corner of his eye.

The bluegrass bar was called Hat Bands, and business was just beginning to pick up for the night. Rows of cars clogged the tiny parking lot, forcing Sandie to look for a space around back.

There was a noise from the back seat as Sandie shut off the engine. The thing had not moved, but its eyes were closed. The noise came again in time with the strains of twelve-string that drifted through the parking lot. It was humming along.

"Better?" Sandie asked. "Do we need to go inside? God, I could use a drink."

The thing thrummed softly, a sound that was almost like a voice.

"Not really," Sandie answered. "I mean, I guess, but it's pretty much just for communicating feelings, unless you use a code..."

Mike frowned hard. The thing in the back fell silent.

"What's it telling you?" he asked.

Sandie rolled down the window to let the music in. In the open yard behind the fence, a fiddle was reeling.

"It wants to know why you're pissed off," she said. "And if you could maybe stop it, because everyone inside is having a good time, and you're kind of ruining it."

"You mean I taste bad?" He shot a glance back at the

dead body, half expecting to see it making a face. Nothing had changed.

"Pretty much, yeah."

Mike bit his lip. "Sandie, this isn't right. Whatever that is, it's not human. We don't know anything about it. I would really rather know what's going on, here..."

"Wouldn't we all?"

Then she was out of the car, adjusting her ponytail and the light jacket she had put on over her tee shirt. She popped open the back door and pulled the creature out, leaving Mike to scramble to catch up.

"You're missing the point," he said at the door. "I'm afraid you're putting yourself in danger. Physical, mental... possibly spiritual."

"Yeah, well, so did the Good Samaritan." Sandie plunged into the bar, dragging her eldritch shadow, bellowing for a beer even as she searched for a table.

"Five years of sleeping through homilies," Mike muttered, wide-eyed, "and that's the bit she manages to pick up..." He rolled up his collar and stuck it into a pocket, trailing after his friend.

The thing sat there glassy-eyed, as still as the salt shaker that seemed to command its attention. It was unnatural, Mike thought, but that only made sense, given what Sandie had told him. What he was seeing was constructed. What was inside was the problem, be it spirit or demon or artificial intelligence. Mike could not even be sure that he believed that there was something inside, but those blind black eyes made it easier to imagine the incredible.

The eyes were what made it hard, Mike decided. Sandie said that the thing was in pain, confused and sick and lost, but the eyes did not show it. The windows to that soul were heavily shuttered. Blackout drapes. If there was anything inside, not a flicker of it showed.

Sandie leaned over. "Hey," she said, half-shouting over the noise from the stage. "Don't worry about it, okay? We'll get this done and get out of here. No problem."

Mike managed a halfhearted smile, but he seriously doubted that. Sandie had gotten herself saddled with far too many stray dogs for him to believe this would be any different.

The thing blinked and moved its spidery, white fingers on the tabletop, probing at the profanities scratched into the wood. PENNY MORALES SWALOWS trailed out from underneath a pale hand. One fingertip followed the lines of the P, picking up some marker and potato chip crumbs as it went.

"Where is it going to go?" Mike asked. "If it's going to heal up or whatever and then you're done with it, where will it go?"

Sandie shrugged. "Dunno. It's got to come from somewhere, right? Maybe it can suck up enough happy to go home."

It did look healthier than it had, or at least as healthy as one could expect from a dead body. The eyes moved occasionally, and it had actually turned its head slightly toward the stage, where two banjos were dueling to the death. Still, Mike did not think that it would be going anywhere any time soon, at least not under its own power. It had barely been able to walk a straight line when they came in, and flying off into outer space or wherever it belonged had to take a lot more energy.

"I'm gonna get a beer," Mike said. Maybe it would help with the urge to run far away from that thing. He stood up and went to the bar rather than flagging down one of the waitresses in the heavy-duty ranch boots; they had a tendency to dangle their winnebagos in one's face, and the last thing he needed was an asthma attack.

"Shiner Bock," he roared at the tiny Hispanic man behind the bar. The man had a panicked look about him, like someone who was very new to the business of bartending. He cupped a hand to his ear and shouted something back, but the drum kit had started up a decidedly non-bluegrass percussion interlude, and placing an order became an exercise in lung capacity.

"*Shiner Bock.*"

"¿Qué?"

"*SHINER. BOCK.*"

"*¿Qué?*"

Mike flapped one hand and pointed at the tap, then traced the silhouette of a bottle in the air with two fingers. The patron next to him was laughing hysterically into her whiskey.

"*SHINERBOCK!*" Mike shrieked as the drum fell silent. Half the bar turned to look at him with understanding grins.

"That's how you know the band is good!" someone called from the corner. He hoped that it had been Sandie.

The band packed up, and a dozen couples vacated the dance floor. A dull throb of conversation picked up to replace the music, and a few people left.

The chalk board by the door said that there was one more band scheduled before closing time, but no band was in evidence. Either way, there were perhaps forty-five more minutes before everyone was kicked out. Forty-five minutes for Sandie to decide how she was going to handle this, whether she was going to leave the thing to fend for itself or commit to keeping it around for an indeterminate length of time. Mike wished that he could be a good shepherd and recommend helping those in need, but that thing just creeped him out too much. He felt an unpleasant conviction that it was eventually just going to up and eat someone.

And when he turned around, it was looking at him. At least, it was looking in his general direction, though with no more focus than ever. Sandie was saying something to it, though he still could not figure out why she talked when it apparently could read her mind. Then he saw an expression on its face, a real expression, one of understanding, and the thing opened up like a twenty-piece ensemble.

It was deafening. The wood floor shook, and the beer in Mike's hand bubbled up and foamed over. It was a perfect encore of the last tune, a fiddle piece with some spiffy mandolin work in the middle, note for note, pitch for pitch, beat for beat – only amplified by a factor of twenty. A few light bulbs exploded.

Every patron ducked and clapped their hands over their ears, and Sandie was shouting, and somehow all three of them got out without being stopped. His ears were still ringing too loudly for him to hear the sirens, but Mike saw red and blue lights racing West down the Loop as they sped away.

In the back seat, the thing looked very lost.

NINE

The creature slumped in a corner of the kitchen. Sandie had told it to sit, and it could not seem to distinguish any practical difference between sitting in a chair and sitting on the floor, so it sat on the floor.

Mike kept an eye on it while Sandie paced. Somehow, it seemed even creepier now that he knew it was both a dead body and a vaguely person-shaped amp. Dead things should not be that loud.

"Okay," Sandie was saying – very loudly, since two thirds of those present were still half-deaf. "Okay, weird is not necessarily bad, but within limits, you know? That was bad. No, trust me. Attracting attention for being weird is a recipe for disaster. I mean, people can't make the same sounds as a whole band." She sighed and yanked hard on her ponytail. "It would help if you could just learn to talk…"

The thing thrummed softly.

Mike cut in. "You're going to keep it? I mean, it probably doesn't eat much, but you're going to have to take care of it somehow, and you can't take it to work, and you can't just leave it here by itself, and I sure can't look after it..."

The thing's eyes swiveled toward him when he talked. It was creepy, but also somehow more normal, like it was making an effort to seem human. Mike was not sure whether to be relieved or disconcerted by that fact. *Extremely realistic*, his mind said sardonically.

Sandie shrugged. "It was on its own when it showed up. I think it would probably do okay at the house. I mean, if we set some ground rules and it doesn't go outside or set the place on fire."

"We still don't know what it is! That would go a long way toward figuring out what to do with it, but we don't know."

"So? It's not like anyone else would know what to do with it, either. I don't want it getting... I dunno, dissected or anything."

The thing sat in the middle of the discussion like a sack of flour, white and smooth and bland. It glanced up at the ceiling fan, and the ceiling fan *vibrated*, shaking down motes of dust into Mike's eyes.

"It's creepy."

"Well... No, okay, I'll give you that one. It's creepy. But so are those hairless cats, and I wouldn't let one of them just wander around lost, either. Or get dissected."

"Cats don't get into your head and read your mind or follow you around in your dreams like some kind of psychic stalker."

"Says you."

"I'm not joking."

"We'll just see, okay? And anyway, kicking it out wouldn't get it out of my head if it's really determined to stay there. And if it really freaks you out so much, d'you think pissing it off might be a bad idea?"

=

Pissing it off might have been a bad idea, but taking it to work was a worse one.

"Cousin," she told Brandon brusquely as she shrugged her apron on and adjusted her name tag.

"How is your cousin *white*?" he wanted to know.

"Hey, now, don't be racist. He's got some problems, okay?"

"He?"

"Yeah, he. I said he's got problems, now leave 'im alone."

The cousin occupied a corner of the Joe Haus and stared out the window toward the highway, where a few thousand panicked San Antonians were hurtling toward the daily grind just a few minutes late. One split off and came hurtling toward the coffee shop, pausing for a moment to extrude Connie before shooting away again toward downtown. The cousin watched impassively.

Connie flopped artistically into the shop, dumped her purse on the counter, and spent a good fifteen seconds staring blank-faced at the thing sitting in the corner. It stared back until she flopped herself into the back to get her apron.

"Mm?" she demanded, falling short of eloquence.

"Yeah," Sandie confirmed in a whisper. "Just go with it, okay? I'm still figuring things out. 'S my 'cousin,' okay?"

"What are you talking about? Who is that actually?"

"That's him. It. That's the zombie."

"Say what, now? I thought it was supposed to be a dead body?"

"Yeah, well, things changed. It's still dead, by the way. Just... upright."

"*¡Mentira!*"

"No, de verdad. Look, I'll update you later, okay? During lunch break or something. When Mike comes."

Connie popped her gum in disbelief and shook her head as she scooted out to start taking orders. Sandie scooted out after her. The shop was beginning to fill up, but a wide open space radiated out from the corner

58

where the thing was sitting. She could hear it humming along with the ambience music, thankfully just a hum and nothing more complex. It still did not sound human, more like an electric keyboard or a particularly well-tuned kazoo, but everyone seemed to be glancing up at the speakers in the ceiling rather than over at the person-shaped amp. It was learning.

Then her attention was arrested by a business suit with a yen for iced mocha, and for the rest of the morning rush, the problem of her counterfeit cousin was pushed onto the back burner. She made a few more mochas, lots of lattes, and a hot chocolate. There were house blends, Columbian black, and a chai tea. Finally, the flood slowed to a gush, the gush to a stream, the stream to a trickle, and Sandie took a moment to grab herself a bottle of water from the back.

In a whisper, she told Connie as much as she dared, until Connie's mohawk was standing on end, and the unlit cigarette slid off of her lip.

Connie swung her head back and forth, slowly. "That's some bad juju right there. Baaaad."

"Yeah, but what's worse? Helping it out, or blowing it off?"

Connie pressed her lips together tightly and fingered the cluster of medals on their chain at her throat.

"I hear ya," Sandie said. She grabbed a second bottle

of water and moved out to check for customers. What she saw was Brandon's back. He was in the corner, trying to strike up a conversation.

The thing was, to all appearances, ignoring him. It was analyzing a napkin in minute detail, poring over the café's logo with single-minded interest while Sandie's spotty manager tried to make small talk.

"My cousin's autistic," he was saying. "Well, not cousin, exactly. She's like, uh, stepdaughter of my uncle's sister-in-law's second husband. But we're all real close, so..."

The napkin tore, and the thing paused. Sandie caught a flash of surprise, then curiosity. It tore the napkin straight down the middle, completely unaware that Brandon was talking. Then it held the two halves together and thrummed.

"Oh," Brandon said. "Cool trick! I've seen that done with ropes. Never with paper. Still no idea how it's done..."

Sandie stood on tiptoe to see that the napkin was whole again, just as whole as the no-longer-rotting body that was holding it.

"Got a name?"

"John!" Sandie blurted from behind the counter. She regretted it a moment later, but the creature at least had the decency to turn its head at the sound of the name, almost as though it understood. She supposed it might have recognized itself in her thoughts.

"John *Doe*?" Connie hissed under her breath from just inside the back room. "Oh, Jesus..."

"He doesn't talk. I mean, you've figured that out. Like I said. Problems. His name's John."

God, why can't you just talk and be normal so I don't start blabbering like an idiot and freak out my boss...

"John," it said clearly, vibrating like the string of a violin. Its mouth did not move. "Like I said. Problems." The voice was Sandie's.

TEN

Sandie made an effort to swallow her shock before Brandon could see. Connie was not as subtle.

"Holy crap," said Connie.

"Holy crap," said John Doe.

"What kind of problems are we talking about?" said Brandon, backing a step away.

"What kind of problems are we talking about?" said John Doe, recoiling from the sudden rush of mistrust.

Please, please stop, Sandie begged silently. The thing met her gaze expressionlessly and set the napkin down on the table. It touched one white forefinger to the sugar shaker, and Sandie could feel a question rising in the mind behind those flat, black eyes.

Later, she whispered. *Not now, later. Please, just don't.*

Connie's knuckles made contact with Sandie's arm,

and she realized that Brandon had asked her something.

"I don't know," she replied without really knowing what the question had been. "It's... He's never done that before."

Brandon shook his head carefully. "Shouldn't you, like, tell his doctors, or something?" At least he seemed to be rolling with the cousin story.

The floor tiles seemed to suck at Sandie's feet, but she made herself take a step toward the back room. The light seemed too bright. She took a long, slow breath.

"Yeah. Yeah, thanks, Brandon. I'll take him home and call them up."

She took him to Our Lady of the Hills, instead. She shoved him up the sidewalk, beneath the towering, twisted live oaks, and into the nave. One the dais beside the altar, a wispy old woman with blued hair was practicing the piano. John echoed a few of the notes, and Sandie could feel the tones vibrating through the thing's smooth, white palm.

"Don't you dare," Sandie hissed, though frankly she was just relieved that it had not burst into flame or anything inside the church.

John fell silent. *unsatisfactory*, it sent. *unpleasant. strong, negative. why?*

Because, - Sandie dragged it up the side aisle and back behind the altar, ignoring the old woman's startled squawk of protest - *you scared the crap out of them. Me, too. I swear, if you ever take my voice again, I will leave you to fend for yourself.*

then how?

Find your own voice. Or shut up and be mute, I don't care, but don't take mine. Sandie realized that she was scared, scared and John was not sucking it away. He disliked it. That made her feel a little bit better, that at least he was not doing it on purpose.

Even so, she found herself hammering just a little bit harder than necessary at the door of the rectory, and Monsignor Grigorio did not look happy when he answered.

The senior priest was almost as big around as he was tall. Even through his black beard, his face was purple. He stood there in sweat pants and a flowery Hawaiian shirt, looming as aggressively as a five-foot man can.

"What the hell?" he demanded, rather appropriately.

"I need Mike," Sandie managed to gasp, so Grigorio planted her on one end of the couch and John on the other and told them to wait. They waited an hour before Mike arrived in collar and cassock, worn out as only an ICU visit could make him. He dropped his briefcase by the door, met Sandie's eyes with a dull stare, and disappeared for a moment into the kitchen. Something inside the briefcase sloshed – Oil, Sandie thought with a blunt pang of nausea. There was the clangor of a mighty battle from the kitchen, and Mike emerged victorious, bearing a tall glass of milk.

The look on his face made Sandie seriously doubt the importance of her own problems.

"Drunk driver," Mike said, sitting down on the end of the coffee table. He closed his eyes and fingered the etching on the side of his glass. "Kid on a bike." Sandie's heart sank. "Six hours. I could really use a nap. Maybe a Tylenol and then a nap. So, what's up with you?"

A lawn mower buzzed somewhere down the block, and the ceiling fan clanked. A bee shrilled angrily from between the window glass and the screen.

The thing sat silently, its blank eyes glued to the blank television screen. It did not speak, or imitate, or whatever that had been. From the look of it, it did not plan to do it again, just as Sandie had ordered.

"Mike, do you want to talk? I mean..."

"Not really. Probably shouldn't, anyway. Professional confidentiality. That and I don't want to."

"Oh. I..." Sandie bit her lip. She did not understand, and she knew it, so she did not say it. "Okay."

Mike blew out a breath and opened his eyes. "So, what's up with you?"

"Not much," Sandie admitted as she realized it was true. "I just... It can talk. Sort of. The same way it did the band. It did my voice, too, and Brandon's, and Connie's. Sort of freaked me out..."

"No damage?"

"No damage."

"Well, that's good, isn't it?"

"I... I'm not sure. You know, you hear someone talking with your voice, and it sort of feels like they've stolen part of you."

"But you haven't lost anything, have you?"

"No."

Mike swallowed the rest of his milk and sat forward. "Ever use a language tape?"

"Huh-uh."

"They do it like that, have you repeat after a native speaker. That's how you learn a language."

"You think?"

"We can hope."

John gave Sandie a sideways glance.

"Is that what you're doing?" she asked.

It only blinked at her.

"Teach it," Mike suggested.

But it was slow going. John listened, repeated sometimes, asked questions, but never really understood. After about a week, he filled his lungs, opened his mouth, and let out a long, zombie-like "Uuuuuhhgh." Sandie congratulated him.

"Can you keep doing that?" she asked. "Breathe in and out? Most people do that all the time."

John breathed in and out.

Sandie set him up in front of the television and went to work. When she came home, he was humming the theme music from the morning news.

"Good morning, San Antonio!" he said cheerily, with the female newscaster's voice.

"Good afternoon," Sandie corrected.

She took him to the movies and let him suck up some corny chick-flick, along with all the accompanying corny chick-flick feelings. After another couple of days, he let her know that he had figured out a way to stand out less, and at the same time use less energy. Sandie was confused until he pointed out his new set of chemical reactions with a hint of something that might have been pride. The only problem was, he continued, that the reactions did not seem to be self-sustaining. Sandie gave him a bowl of macaroni and showed him how to work a fork. Life suddenly became a bit more expensive as it became necessary to feed two instead of one.

"What do you think about getting a job?" Sandie asked over a meal of ramen noodles and eggs.

The sounds of the Java Haus flashed into her head,

cups and talk and the rumble of the coffee grinder. John tilted his head.

"I don't know," she said. "Maybe you could learn to make coffee. But you've really, really got to learn to talk, first. I mean, the breathing was a good start. That and the being alive..." She had not told Mike about that part, not knowing for sure what a priest would make of a self-resurrecting-zombie-amplifier.

John sent her babble and noise. Chaos.

"I know. I know it doesn't make sense, but I promise you, there are rules, and you can learn them. You just need practice."

He thrummed. *noise and tone. tone and pitch. frequency. logical. efficient.*

"Yeah, I know. But that's not how we talk to each other."

music. jazzbluegrass transmit meaning deep meaning feeling.

"Meaning, yeah. But not all the meanings. Like if I wanted to tell you to do something, or tell you how to do something, or tell you my name, I couldn't do that with music."

name. He tilted his head. "John." He still used her voice, the same voice she had used the first time, stiff and breathless and a little bit desperate. He said it as a statement, as she had, but there was a question underneath.

"I don't know your actual name."

He said nothing back, aloud or silently, just probed at the soup with his weird sort of sonar. The surface of the soup rippled, and the noodles squirmed.

"You don't know either, do you?"

you call me John. not actual real true natural?

Sandie thought about that as she got up to pour two glasses of water from the kitchen sink. The city water came up from the aquifer loaded with minerals that ruined hardware but tasted good. Tiny bubbles swirled in the glass. She could feel John's eyes on her back and his attention on what she was doing. He was getting better at that, at watching with his eyes instead of with whatever strange psychic thing he had going on. She was not sure why she assumed that an inhuman creature should have something as normal as a name. Maybe it had never had one. Maybe that was part of the damage she could sense in its mind.

"Actually... Actually, wait. Hang on a second."

She ran upstairs and dragged a drooping cardboard box out of the attic, grabbed the thing that was sitting on top, and ran back down.

John took the gift gingerly, with more perplexity than gratitude. It left dust on his fingers, and he looked up at the echo of distaste in Sandie's brain.

"It belonged to my ex," she explained. "Still does, I guess. But if he ever wants it back, he'll have to get rid of those photos first... Never mind. It's out of tune, probably. But I bet Mike could teach you. He plays a little bit..."

John laid one white finger on the guitar's pick-guard. He turned his attention downward, and the strings resonated in cheerful dissonance.

"Like at the bar. If you could learn to make your own music, maybe you could... y'know... get people to feel for you. Whenever you need."

He blinked. Sandie figured it was the closest to a smile he was likely to get.

"You're welcome."

ELEVEN

Connie gnawed pieces out of the end of a ballpoint pen while Sandie tried to explain the situation.

"I mean, I just don't know what to do with him. He seems to have a thing for music, so I figure if he can figure out that guitar, I could maybe set him up with playing it somewhere, but I just can't afford to support a... someone else..."

"So it's a him, now?" Connie interjected, spitting a bit of plastic delicately into her hand. She shoved lavender fingernails through her mohawk and flipped the mass of blue-black hair to the other side of her head, making her earrings jingle.

Sandie made a face. "Well, once I tagged him with 'John Doe,' he sort of had to be a he. I never really realized how much people hang up on gender. So I guess it's just as well, because he couldn't have just stayed an it."

"Okay, so it hasn't actually sprouted dangly bits."

"Connie!"

"Just checking. Seriously, not a whole lot would surprise me at this point."

"Me, neither."

Across the room, John was fingering the chords Mike had shown him the day before. He knew the notes very well, humming them in that strange way he had, vibrating his entire body like a speaker. "Like it's coming from his bones," Mike had commented, and that seemed to Sandie like as good a description as any. When it came to drawing the same notes from a guitar, though, progress came rather more slowly. These fingers did not want to move that precisely, he had complained silently, holding out the resuscitated white flesh as though he expected Sandie could fix it. Moving this matter is hard, and manipulating objects is hard, and there are easier ways to produce frequencies. He had demonstrated, resonating like a full string quartet, but Sandie had shot him down.

"Just trust me," she had begged him. "You have to learn to do it like Mike does it. People in large groups don't like things that are different. It'll cause trouble." She went to the library and picked up a video about the race riots. "And those people were just human beings," she told him.

But film does not capture feelings, and the images on the screen meant nothing to him.

"He's still freaky." Connie slurped at her beer and worried at the tab with her fingernails. "Getting better, though. Sort of cute-freaky. Like a tarsier."

"A what?"

"Tiny primates with eyeballs the size of their brains."

"Big eyeballs or small brains?"

"Both."

John's twanging stopped for a moment, and he looked over at the women with expressionless black eyes. Sandie wondered just how functional his brain was.

"You need to figure out what you're looking for," she told him, "so you can hurry up and find it."

not working. chaos and dissonance. no feeling.

"No, say it out loud."

Connie snorted. "You're like his mother or something." But she still fingered the little cluster of medals at her throat. The favorite of the day seemed to be Saint Michael.

John opened his mouth and groaned like a B-movie zombie.

"Come on, use the muscles, not just air."

"K-k-k-k-khnnnuh."

"Better! That's better! That could almost have been a

75

word."

John blinked and let her know that he still was not sure why his clumsy noises pleased her so much.

"Because practice makes perfect."

He shook his head and rolled his eyes, and Connie almost fell out of her chair laughing. "There," she said. "That right there. You've taught him well, Master Sandie."

"Don't you laugh at me. I'd bet anything he got that from you."

Then he pulled a nearly-recognizable Twinkle Twinkle out of the guitar, and all drinking and banter were put on hold as congratulations were passed around. They celebrated with buttered noodles and garlic toast.

=

After his success, Sandie almost could not get John to put the instrument down. His white fingers spidered away at the frets until well past midnight, with what Sandie might have called dogged determination, if not for his lack of expression.

"Look," she told him at last. "I have no idea whether you actually have to sleep or not, but I do, and I can't while you're making noise."

"Because practice makes perfect," he told her in her own voice, not looking up from his obsession.

Sandie took the guitar away, reamed him out, and

went to bed. But she dreamed that, with nothing to do, he slipped out of the house and went looking for what he had lost. He passed the silent jazz bar, then a spasm of giddy bewilderment that felt to Sandie like a pot house. There was little enough road rage to be had so late at night, so he passed beneath the Anderson Loop, through a dark parking lot, and around one of the countless quarries. She rolled out of bed around five, slipped on an oversized tee shirt, and made damn sure that he was actually gone before scuffing out to the car. She found him standing in an ant bed on the side of I-10, watching the tiny red and black bodies take bits out of his skin.

like this, he told her as she used a blanket to beat the ants off. *like this others knowing/sensing/understanding/hearing/together-being. others.*

Sandie turned him around in the headlights to make sure there were no bugs left. "You say one word about a hive mind," she warned, "and you are outta here, Johnny."

She bundled him into the car and got him home, but home was no better. He stood on the porch and stared into the halogen-lit darkness as though listening hard. His black eyes twitched back and forth, not focusing on anything in particular. She could feel him straining.

"No others," she said gently, taking him by the elbow to get him inside. "Not here, anyway."

we us two?

"Yeah, just us."

He took the news with grace and his usual apathy, but she leaned over to give him a one-armed hug, anyway.

"You're gonna be okay. Promise."

She made him hot chocolate despite the season, on the off-chance that it would help. Then she set him up on the couch and gave back his guitar.

"Just... quietly, please," she told him before heading back to bed to steal whatever minutes she had left until her alarm rang.

She lay down, shut off the light, and closed her eyes. Then she switched the light back on and checked in the closet and under the bed, in case of others.

TWELVE

"Good morning, San Antonio."

It was like no voice Sandie had ever heard before, bizarrely tonal, as though the speaker could not decide whether he was talking or singing. The sounds came slowly, laboriously, elongated by effort and intense concentration.

She rolled over to find the creature standing in the doorway. The voices of morning newscasters drifted up the stairs and down the hall, but those voices were generic and familiar, drained of dialect and character, just like the voice of every other newscaster in America. The one that had woken her was different.

"Lane closures down San Pedro between the Anderson Loop and Sandau Road will continue today. Commuters can expect delays of up to half an hour, so leave early."

"Holy crap!" Sandie sat bolt-upright in bed, tugging absently at her oversized nightshirt. "John, you're doing it!"

The black eyes closed in a slow blink. The bald head canted to one side.

"You have no idea what you're saying, though, do you?"

"Two children went missing from Hollywood Park overnight. Adrianna and Ricardo Hernandez, ages twelve and seven, were last seen camping out in a tent in their back yard around eight PM yesterday evening, but were gone when their father, Mario, went to check on them again around ten. Police are not yet treating the disappearances as a kidnapping."

"That's okay. One thing at a time, huh?"

John blinked again and headed back downstairs, to all appearances unaware of Sandie's excitement. She hastily belted on a bath robe and followed him.

"Were you up all night?"

up.

"I mean, you never went to sleep? Do you sleep?"

practice. always practice get the hang of make muscles for working communication.

"Well, that's good. I mean, this is a huge leap. That was half the problem, right there. Now, if we can just get you to understand it..."

practice makes perfect.

"True. That's true. So... I have work today, but you can keep practicing while I'm gone. Watch the television and repeat after them. Is that how you picked it up?"

imitate small imitate only approximate.

"Yeah, it'll only be close. I mean, everyone's got a different voice. Nobody's is the same as someone else's. Glad you found yours, though. You using mine was creepy."

Sandie poured herself a bowl of corn flakes and filled the coffee maker for the first time in weeks. The smell of it nearly made her gag, after working at the Joe Haus, but late nights demanded caffeine.

John left the kitchen and came back holding his guitar. He touched the strings, but did not strum. As ever, his expression betrayed no feeling, but Sandie received the impression that he was thinking very hard. Of course, she reflected, it was entirely possible that he wanted her to know he was thinking hard.

"Okay," she said, "I'll bite. What's up?"

tone voice order orderly cohesive coherent understand frequency talk?

"I have no idea what you're talking about."

He touched the strings of the guitar, drawing forth a cheerful chord, then echoed the chord in that strange, humming way he had. Then a tiny line appeared between his eyebrows as he visibly decided to do things the hard way.

"Happy birthday to you," he sang slowly, with a glance toward the television in the living room. "Happy birthday to you. Happy birthday, dear Elliot, happy birthday to you."

Sandie wondered for a moment who Elliot might be before realizing that he must have heard it during his television-binge. "You mean singing," she said around a mouthful of corn flakes. "Music?"

music. He sent her a sound-filled impression of the bluegrass bar, with emphasis on the instruments. Guitar, bass, mandolin, fiddle, double-bass, banjo. *tone talk?*

"Yeah, people can make music, too. It's called singing. I mean, you've heard it before. Like, at work. They're always playing songs at the coffee shop, not just instrumentals."

He hummed softly, mimicking the jingle from a local commercial, and wandered back into the living room to plant himself in front of the television.

"Oh, Ignacio," Sandie heard from the other room, "how could I have been so blind for so long? Forgive me, my angel!"

Good enough, she supposed. She finished her cereal, threw on a white tee shirt and black jeans, and pulled her hair back into a ponytail for work.

"Chica," Connie told her when she arrived, "you are in desperate need of some under-eye concealer."

"Late night," Sandie said. "He wandered off and I had to go get him back."

"Couldn't just leave him, huh?"

"Nah. Something would eat him. Or run over him, or something."

Connie popped her gum and flipped her mohawk. There were more rings in her ears than usual. "You're a better woman than me, hermana."

Sandie grinned. "Maybe, but you have more fun."

Mike met them for lunch. It was too hot to eat barbecue in the back of his minivan, so they piled into the back room of the Joe Haus instead. Mike had the presence of mind to bring a roll of paper towels, and they each dropped fifty cents into the jar by the refrigerator, in payment for three stolen cans of soda.

"He's sort of figured out talking. Can't make his own sentences, but if he had, like, a repertoire or something of phrases, maybe. Doesn't quite sound normal, though. I can't put my finger on it. It's like he's still doing the humming thing, only he's not."

"Hey, progress is progress," said Mike, whose creased forehead betrayed his real thoughts on the matter. "Next thing you know, he'll be virtually human."

"Pfff," said Connie. "Yeah, when pigs fly. Virtually

human, my tight brown ass. No, see," – she leaned forward with a knowing nod – "you need to get him into show biz. That would be one frigging awesome gimmick, you know? It would be like, woooo, space alien who plays guitar but never talks. And he'd be famous just for being freaky, 'cause everybody's into that jazz."

"Yeah, sure. Maybe once he can play guitar."

Mike bought a latte and hung around in the corner for the rest of the day, his pager and a memo book laid out neatly beside his mug. "I'm following you home," he told Sandie. "I'm going to be teaching this divinity course online, and I want to run my first lecture by you before I film it. And maybe you could show me how to work a webcam." He grinned and wiggled his eyebrows. "You know."

Sandie hung up her apron at five o'clock, handed Brandon the keys to the espresso machine, and crawled into her car. She spared a moment to worry about John alone at the house, but he had not blown anything up yet, and it seemed unlikely that he would wander away again, and even if he did, she knew she could probably find him. She drove home with Mike close on her tail.

The house was still there when she arrived, and she could see John sitting on the couch through the open blinds. She pulled into the garage, leaving the door open so Mike could follow her in.

Something stopped her, though, just before she put

her hand on the doorknob that would take her into the rest of the house. There was sound from inside, something she did not think should be coming from a television. The hair on her arms lifted.

"John?" she asked quietly. No one else in the world could have heard her through the door, over whatever that sound was, but she knew that he would. Sound was his domain, after all. She pushed the door open, and the vibrations washed over her, settled into a lump in her throat, brought tears to her eyes. Something inside her broke free and soared.

"Oh, God," she choked.

THIRTEEN

A half-step behind Sandie, Mike heard it, too.

And it was mind-blowing. It sounded like angels, he thought, but he knew better than that. There was a far more down-to-earth explanation sitting on the couch – or at least, a more tangible one, he corrected himself. There were goose bumps on his arms and a shiver deep inside his spine, a sense of something not quite right. Still, he let himself stop in the doorway to listen, and for a moment, just a moment, he let himself fly.

Then the sound stopped, and that thing was standing at the end of the hall, its bald head cocked to one side, staring at them through impassive black eyes. The elation began to ebb, and Mike shook himself, entertaining a sneaking suspicion that John Doe was sucking up his happiness like a sponge. That was fair enough, he supposed; it was not really his in the first place.

"Damn," Sandie whispered with a kind of dazed reverence.

Mike looked over to see tears in her eyes. She wiped them away hastily with the back of her hand. He could sympathize, though; that was pretty much his exact sentiment.

"Damn," she said again, and she rushed forward to seize that thing's hand and drag it back into the living room.

Mike followed, which was pretty much the only thing he could do. He fell onto the couch, realizing a moment later that he was sitting almost exactly where the creature had been earlier, and put a moment's serious thought into moving to a chair. Good Samaritan, he reminded himself. Helping creepy things is good, is right. He stayed put.

"What was that?" Sandie was demanding, even though by her own admission, the thing did not so much understand her words as pick up on her thoughts.

"Singing," it said quietly. The word was a statement, but the tilt of its head was a question, and it did not take much imagination to identify that weird, mechanical voice as the one that had greeted them when they arrived.

"Well, yeah," said Sandie, "but..." She trailed off, shaking her head, and plopped herself down beside Mike. Mike shook his head, too.

"Weird," he said, and then, at a glare from Sandie, he

amended: "But... kind of cool. And progress. I guess. Actually talking, that's good." He pulled his collar off, rolled it up, and stuck it in his pocket. He could not be sure, but he thought that might be a nervous habit.

"And handy," Sandie added. "I mean, if you can just... make..." She broke off, biting her lip.

John only stood there. It blinked once, slowly.

"Efficient, yeah," Sandie answered.

"Efficient," the thing repeated in its weird voice.

"But how does that help?" Mike broke in. He stood up to look the thing in the eye. "You're looking for something, right? Something that's apparently pretty hard to find? How does this help?"

It tipped its head to one side and glanced at Sandie.

"He says it makes it easier to think," she said. "If he can make his own food, he doesn't have to waste time looking for it. And it's easier to think when he's not hungry. And bear in mind, that's basically nothing but crappy analogy, because I have no idea what the right words would actually be."

Its eyes moved across the room, focusing for a moment on the back door, then on Mike, then on the table lamp.

"And he knows that he made you upset, and he wants to know why, so whatever it is, he won't do it again."

"Seriously?"

"Well, basically. You gotta understand, this whole thing isn't exactly, uh, conducive to being precise. But he really wants you to not be pissed off."

"Because it, what, tastes bad?"

"Yeah, pretty much."

Mike shook his head and gave the creature a long minute of intense examination. It kept its face turned away from him, focus fixed on the dark table lamp. If the lamp turned on by itself, Mike decided, he was just going to get up and leave.

But on the other hand, he had heard it, and – more importantly – he had felt it, and someone had told him long ago that music was the language of angels. Whatever that bald and creepy creature was, it knew how to create joy. It was joy, he realized; even though he had only had a second to feel it, there was no mistaking that calm, that sense of passing beyond the mundane. Whether it was hollow and false, some kind of trick... Well, that remained to be seen. He pressed his fingertips to his lips and shrugged expressively.

"I really don't think I can offer a professional opinion on this," he admitted to himself and to Sandie, "and I'm kind of reluctant to ask. The Monsignor wouldn't... well, I'd hazard a guess that he wouldn't know what to do with... any of this."

He left without rehearsing his lecture, still pursued

by the feeling that he should be doing something to help. Leaving Sandie alone to be manipulated by that thing felt wrong, even though there was no reason to assume that John Doe was nursing any nefarious plans. The streets were dark and silent, oddly so for nine o'clock at night. He took Vance Jackson to Huebner and passed beneath I-10 with a mumbled prayer for guidance.

"I am not a bad priest," he told the rear-view mirror. "I just need to figure out whether this is a welcome-the-stranger thing or a protect-the-flock thing. I could really use a sign, about now."

And behold, a sign appeared. Mike, distracted, drove straight past it without noticing, but the traffic cop noticed and turned on his lights.

"Didn't see that stop sign, Father?" the officer asked, tapping his motorcycle boots with all the impatience of a man stuck on a late patrol. He issued a warning, only a warning.

Mike glanced up as he pulled back onto the street. "Stop sign," he muttered. "Yeah, real funny."

FOURTEEN

Sandie dreamed of heat, intense heat, something shrill and damaging, and the knowledge of her own impending destruction. She dreamed of silence, holding tight to the belief that once there had been harmony, that something now forgotten had come before. She dreamed that she was not born in fire and pain.

She woke without tears, understanding that her dreams came from a place that did not feel.

John met her on the stairs as she came down to check on him.

"Trying to remember?" she asked.

He nodded. *rethink and rethink and rethink always never before the shriek.* He held his guitar like a safety blanket but did not touch the strings.

"That's the first thing you remember?"

He nodded again. *consider genesis generative force creation first memory of beginning.* But that did not seem right. There had to be something before that, something that built a framework of understanding long before this hard, remote world came smashing in with its confusion. He had to have been used to something once, or else why would everything seem so unfamiliar? *contrast deep contrast but always two at least two.*

"Don't push it, okay? Either it'll come back to you, or it won't. Don't stress yourself out."

She was more stressed than he was, though. He gave her a look that was almost sly and sang, pianissimo, a few notes that she knew had been special to her, once. The anxiety vanished, replaced by an echo of the previous night's euphoria. You shouldn't do that, she wanted to tell him, but she could not. Instead, she called Brandon with an apology and an excuse.

"I've got an idea," she told John as she hung up the phone. She piled him into the car and dragged him to the south side of town, taking US 281 at a speed that would have made Mike ill.

She pulled into the parking lot of a creepy little dive with blackwashed cinderblock walls and green-painted plywood nailed over the windows. Early in the morning, the place looked deserted. There was no one else in the parking lot, and the single security light affixed above the blackwashed door did not turn on as they approached.

The sign beneath said "Please leave all preconceptions outside." Sandie hammered on the door anyway, producing a clang of metal.

"Nacho!" she bellowed at the rusted knob. "Nacho, get up! I brought you something! Up, Nacho! I found your sound!"

The ringing of the steel door slowly died away, and someone's edger started up in a lawn nearby. A small, yappy dog took issue with the noise and added his complaints to the din. John hummed uncertainly.

Then a postmodern beatnik oozed around the side of the building.

"I'm up," said Nacho. He adjusted the lapels of his sleek, black linen suit, smoothed down one high, arched eyebrow, and regarded Sandie imperiously over the tops of slim, utilitarian spectacles. "It's always evening here in the Zone. We haven't seen *you* around here in ages, darling. I was beginning to think you must have gone prosie on us."

"Well, you know, there was stuff..."

"Your parents."

"... and verses don't make much money..."

"How plebeian."

"... and we had our own issues..."

"Personal issues. You didn't need to stop coming. The others didn't understand."

"... and it just seemed easier."

"And yet you come bearing gifts." Nacho raised one forefinger and ran a nail thoughtfully over the small patch of glossy black hair that separated his lip and chin. He darted only a glance at John and wordlessly beckoned the two to follow him around the side of the building and in through a side door.

Inside, the creepy little dive was transformed. The cinderblock walls were hung with thick, black carpeting, studded with shaded sconces that threw a murky, golden light on the parlor – parlor was the only possible word. Heavy wingback chairs in two dozen mismatched styles surrounded low, bare tables that all crowded around a circular dais in the middle of the room. The dais was empty for the moment, but Sandie knew that somewhere in the back rooms were a grand piano and a large assortment of stools and props. The large assortment of drinks was locked in glass-fronted cabinets against one wall.

Sandie felt for John and felt him feeling for someone else. She squinted through the low light and found four other people, all women, watching her from across the room. Two of them smiled, one only stared, and the fourth scrambled for a notebook from her purse.

"Don't mind them." Nacho picked up a glass of water and took a sip. "We were discussing an event – You're welcome to come, by the way, if you need money. It's a sort of a competition. Now, what did you say you'd found?"

"Your sound," Sandie said. "How did you put it? 'The auditory coalescence of human sentiment?' I found it, and I'm feeding it, and it needs a job."

"Your rather remarkable friend, here? Good voice?"

"You could probably say that."

"Could I?"

"Do you believe in magic?"

"Convince me."

Sandie turned to John, who had moved away by a few steps and was watching the small bevy of women with intense concentration but little real interest.

"Do it again," she said, "like last night."

A pencil, a notebook, and a glass of water hit the plush carpet in almost perfect unison. A spray of droplets pattered unnoticed against the speechless proprietor's perfect shoes. What happened next was lost.

A minute or five minutes or half an hour later, Nacho blinked, swallowed hard, and nodded. One of the women went fishing in her purse for tissues. Sandie pulled herself together and folded her arms with a glance at John, who was discreetly soaking up what was left of the emotional chaos he had created.

"Explain?" Nacho demanded. He raised a hand and

smoothed his moustache with a quick, convulsive motion.

"Can't," Sandie said. "But I'd hazard a guess that the bar tips after an hour of that would be astronomical."

"Can't argue with that. You guys..." – he flapped one hand at the women with a look of intense distraction – "...carry on. Or go on home. We got enough done, I think, and this... I'll need to take a closer look at this." He turned on his heel, leaving his spilt glass of water exactly where it was, circled around a few tables to the back wall, and disappeared behind a hanging rug.

Sandie grabbed John by the hand, took a last look at Nacho's somewhat dazed focus group, and hurried back to join him in his secret lair.

The secret lair was a grey, linoleum-lined kitchen. Nacho and his perfect hair and spotless suit were about as out of place as anything could be, but he plopped into a wire-and-pleather kitchen chair all the same and pushed his glasses up onto the top of his head.

"What exactly are you wanting?" he asked. He pulled out his neat, black pocket square and dabbed at his lip, then smoothed his moustache again. "You said a job? And what exactly is..." There was a pause as he struggled for a pronoun. "I mean, what exactly is his deal? His, right? Some kind of savant or something?"

He turned to John with a helpless look, the tips of his

ears going faintly red. "Don't you talk, or anything?"

John looked back without expression and blinked his flat, black eyes, and Nacho visibly suppressed a shudder.

"No, he doesn't talk." Sandie drew up her own chair and motioned for John to do the same. "I can't really explain that, either. Mostly because I just don't know, right? I'm not keeping secrets or anything. Anyway, he came to me, and I'm taking care of him, and I can't afford it, and he's got a marketable skill, and I think hanging out around lots of people would be good for him. You could let him sing here, or I know you've got other friends looking for something, if you know of a gig anywhere..."

"Are you kidding me? He'd cause a riot."

"Don't be stupid. Do you feel like rioting right now?"

"More like closing this place down, drinking enough coffee to keep me up for the rest of my life, and desperately working on achieving what he has."

"Motivated, right? Kind of optimistic? Like you can take on everything?"

"Yeah, that's pretty close."

Sandie leaned back and crossed her legs, making her chair squeak. "So, do you have something?"

"Give me a week, okay? I don't have much of a crowd ordinarily, so I'll have to do some calling around to make it into an event. I can only hold maybe fifty in here, if we really squeeze them in, so I'll make sure it'll be interested parties. I know some restaurant owners, bar owners – I mean, I'd love to have him weekly or something if it works out, but my regulars don't really tip, and you said you wanted money."

Nacho darted a furtive glance at the silent singer staring at the boarded-up window.

"He's not some kind of incompetent, or anything? Legal stuff, you know. You can't just scrape some poor guy off the street and put him to work. This isn't like that dog you picked up that one time? Or the parrot? Or the skunk?"

"No, he came to me. Stood there on my back porch until I let him in. Then last night, he did... that. He likes it. It's hard to explain. As for legal stuff, hiring is probably going to be a problem. No papers, no social, not even a name, really."

"Legal nonentity, right. So cash gigs only, no contracts. Sandie, I know you wouldn't be unscrupulous, but... I mean, you don't even know his name?"

"To be perfectly honest, I don't even know if he's..." Sandie bit her lip and shifted in her chair, quickly reassessing the amount of trust she was willing to give. "I call him John. Like John Doe. He's damaged, yeah. Amnesia, or something. Something happened to him. But look, he wants to figure himself out, and I think this is his way of doing that. And maybe if we can raise enough, we can afford tests or something, find out what's wrong with him and maybe fix it."

"Well, and start checking for missing persons reports and stuff. People don't just show up without having disappeared from some place, first."

"Yeah. Yeah. But you'll help?"

"I'll help."

"Thanks, Nacho." Sandie leaned forward to plant a quick kiss on his cheek, even though that felt manipulative and wrong. Fortunately, he barely seemed to notice.

"You found the sound. I can't believe you found the sound."

FIFTEEN

Connie hooked one arm around Mike's shoulders. If it had been anyone else, he would have had to object, but Connie was the sort to brook no objection. Her mohawk was gelled upright for the occasion, stained red and saturated with glitter to complement her sparkling nose ring, brow rings, and two dozen earrings. Her blue leather jacket creaked and crackled against the black leather sofa. Her fingernails were the same red as her hair, and they tapped out a pattern on Mike's shoulder.

Mike put up with it. He had ironed his pants and his shirt and polished his shoes, but that was about it. His pasty face and blond hair showed up in the low, yellow light, but the rest of him vanished into the couch. He edged an inch or two away from Connie, partly because San Antonio was not big enough to ensure that he would not run into a parishioner and partly because the spikes on her belt were digging into his hip.

"Ow," he said.

"Oh, man up," Connie returned.

Somewhere in the back, Sandie and John were lurking. They had been whisked away by a strange, postmodern beatnik almost as soon as they had stepped out of the car, while another of that peculiar breed had appeared moments later to foist coffee on Connie and Mike. The first had been a man in shining custom cowboy boots and the obligatory black turtleneck, a pencil-thin line of black hair adorning his upper lip, the lower playing host to a dime-sized patch of the same. The second was a person much like John – that is to say, thin and of indeterminate gender – in a button-down and fake glasses. That one had also disappeared after giving each of the low tables a thorough wipe down.

And for two hours, nothing happened. Mike read an eBook, some of the lighter works of GK Chesterton, and Connie slept on the arm of the couch. The second beatnik flitted in and out, making minute adjustments to the lighting, shoving pieces of furniture around, and finally wheeling a mobile bar out of the back rooms.

"Shouldn't someone be getting here soon?" Mike had asked.

The beatnik had smiled and pushed eir hair back into a ponytail. "Don't worry," ey said. "There are cars outside.

They just haven't come in, yet."

"Why not?"

"It's all a matter of headspace, of course. You have to be in the right one before you enter the Zone."

"What sort of headspace, exactly?"

"Oh, don't worry, Padre. You're smooth." A sage nod accompanied that statement, and ey disappeared into the back once again.

Mike took a wild guess that *smooth* was probably a good thing.

Amazingly, the first three who wandered in were normal people. One was bald, one wore jeans, and the third trailed a cloud of cigarette smoke, which Mike thought probably explained the lure of the parking lot much better than any metaphysical speculation on headspace. The fourth, following scarce minutes behind, was only barely an adult; and the fifth was a Van Gogh lookalike.

Another half hour later, the Zone was full.

"See?" asked Connie, who had come awake early enough to touch up her hair and cobalt-blue lipstick. "See? This is going to be so badass. I told you guys, didn't I? Rock star. For the win."

"It's not something you'll ever forget," Mike said, keeping his concerns to himself. Connie was excited, and Sandie was excited, and the pomo beatnik man was excited. Even John, though by no means excited, seemed more engaged than usual, more determined to react correctly and blend in as much as possible. As much as Mike was tempted to be a downer, he just could not bring himself to do it. *Faith, hope, and love,* he reminded himself. *Faith in people, hope that everything goes smoothly tonight, love that transcends creepiness.*

The lights directly above the dais brightened slowly, until Mike realized that it was Sandie standing there. She looked pretty good, in a managerial sort of way, with her hair pulled back in a bun and her sensible shoes planted squarely beneath billows of green cotton skirt.

"Hey, everybody," she said. "I'm Sandie Melindrez. Some of you probably remember me from a couple of years ago when I used to come to slams here. I haven't been back in a while, but now I'm here for a friend, John, who is probably the most incredible thing you'll ever hear. And, uh... Sorry, I suck at intros. Anyway, we want to thank Nacho - Sorry, Ignacio. You all know Ignacio. Anyway, we want to thank Ignacio Villalobos for letting us use his Zone and helping us put this whole thing together for tonight."

There was a smattering of uncertain applause. Connie poked Mike hard in the chest.

"This is it!" she hissed.

Mike nodded and tried to will the knots out of his stomach. He did not stick his fingers in his ears, even though the thought was tempting.

"Anyway," Sandie said once more, "this may sound a little odd, but I'd like to ask anyone standing to sit now, and if you're holding anything, I'm going to need you to put it down." She smiled and tucked a wisp of hair behind her ear. "Artists are allowed to make strange requests, right?"

She stepped down, and John stepped up. He was holding a microphone, but it did not take a genius to tell that he had no idea what to do with it. It stayed close to his side, nowhere near his mouth. It was a good thing that the Zone was small, because the microphone was going to be useless. On the other hand, John had not seemed to have any problem with volume in the past. That one time at the bluegrass bar came to mind.

Mike swallowed hard and felt Connie elbow him in the side.

"Loosen up," she whispered.

But John was looking at him, only at him, and that made loosening up difficult. Sandie seemed to think that the creepy thing had no feelings to be hurt, but Mike felt bad all the same. *Sorry*, he thought as hard as he could, and tried to stop freaking out. It did not work.

Then it happened again. John sucked in a breath, his narrow chest expanding visibly, and when he let it out again, everything stopped. Sandie had picked out a selection of folk songs in English and Spanish, a couple of heart-wrenching tear-jerkers from Ireland, and some old jazz-age bits that would work a cappella. Mike did not hear a single word. He was lost, and so was everyone else in the Zone. The place could have caught fire, and no one would have noticed.

The set was one hour long. Sandie had timed all of the songs, and she had said that John was pretty damned good about imitating things with precision, so if he ploughed straight through, it would take him almost exactly one hour. It was just about an hour later, then, that the room woke up.

Nothing moved. Connie uttered a breathy little gasp, and someone across the room coughed delicately. Mike opened his eyes, though he could not remember having shut them, and he leaned forward to pick up his coffee. It was cold.

He could still feel it in his bones, the way the sounds suddenly made sense and his doubts evaporated. He could feel it as though it had been real, no matter how much reason cautioned him against convincing illusions. The high was still with him, full of promise and surety.

Sandie plopped down on the couch beside him. "You don't ever get used to it," she said quietly. She looked satisfied, and Mike could understand why; four people oozing importance were making their way through the maze of chairs toward the Nacho person, and all four of them were pulling out business cards.

"Damn," Connie whispered. "Damn, girl, you tried to warn me. That was... I mean, damn. He's like walking pot."

"Not exactly how I would have put it, but yeah."

John was still standing in the middle of the dais, caught in his little circle of light, the microphone dangling from white fingers. He turned and met Mike's gaze, and the flat black eyes crinkled in a startling expression.

He smiled.

SIXTEEN

The smile had surprised him, but Mike got over it. He was starting to get an inkling of something, something that would explain a lot. He hesitated to think too hard on it, though; it is a capital mistake to theorize without data.

He looked around. Connie had found herself a drink somewhere and was chatting up the nongendered beatnik, who had ditched the fake glasses and picked up a small fedora. Sandie and the Nacho person had moved off to talk business with a woman whose shirt urged readers to "Eat At Mag's." A low murmur had sprung up in the Zone, but still, everyone remained mostly seated. It looked as though no one could work out an appropriate reaction to what they had just heard.

John, meanwhile, had been forgotten. He stood still on the dais, bathed in a halo of dull, yellow light, the microphone still dangling from his fingers. No one had told him to move.

This time, Mike could see the confusion on the creature's face, even though it was little more than a faint tightening of the smooth, white forehead, a quick twitch of the black eyes.

"Love of God," he muttered, pushing himself up from the couch. He wriggled between two more sofas and a table, stepped over a woman's feet, and finally got close enough to touch John's hand; the skin was warm, and for some strange reason, that creeped Mike out all the more, since it was unexpected. The creature looked down at him.

"Why don't you come sit down?" he suggested, pointing to the couch and miming sitting.

John did not even blink.

"Sit?" Mike tried again. "You could come sit with me. Here." He reached out and took the microphone and set it on the edge of the platform. John let it go without resistance.

"C'mon." Mike took a step back toward the couch, but John did not follow. "C'mon? Oh, come on. You're being all sad, and it's making me nervous." He grabbed John's hand and gave it a tug. John followed.

"There, better. No reason to stand around and make things awkward." The two made their way back to the couch where Connie and her new squeeze were squeezing. Mike pulled, and John followed. After another brief flurry of failed communication, the two sat.

Connie reached across Mike to poke John in the ribs. "You," she said, "were awesome. That was awesome. You're going to make a CD, and I want a copy. Lots of copies. I so told you so. I told everybody."

"Bwahahahahaha," Mike interjected drily.

Connie raised her arm and elbowed him in the chest. "Don't be a jerk. I did say so. And if anyone here is going to go supervillain, I think it should be Nacho. He's already got the 'stache. I'll just write his monologues for him."

"And then everyone will see?"

"Totes."

"Sounds like a good plan."

John moved suddenly, looking up, and a moment later, a woman's hand appeared in front of his face.

"Jen Stratford," she shot, while John blinked at her multitude of rings. "You've got a pretty remarkable talent, kid. I've got a place out west side of the Connelly Loop, be interested in seein' ya there in the near future."

Mike felt Connie tense beside him and sensed more than saw Sandie freaking out from halfway across the room. Something thudded. He guessed that Sandie had tripped over a chair.

"He doesn't really talk," Mike said, since no one else seemed to know how to handle the situation. "He's sort of special. What you might call a savant."

Jen Stratford's sparkly hand withdrew. "Oh, right," she said a little too loudly. "Like autism or something."

"Or something," Mike agreed truthfully enough, even though her bluntness balked him.

"Hey," she said, putting up her hands defensively, as though she sensed that she might have caused offense, "I'm as equal-opportunity as anyone. If he can do the job, that's that."

Mike only shrugged. "I'm not handling that," he said. "Sandie's his agent."

"Thank you," John said quietly. His attention seemed fixed on one of the dim ceiling lights. Mike, Connie, and Jen paused for a moment, waiting to see if he would go on, but he did not.

Jen Stratford nodded knowingly, and Mike found himself inexplicably pissed off. He took her business card anyway, for the sake of politeness.

"I would be very happy to offer a position," she said, smiling, and she walked away to visit with the competition.

"Everything okay?" Sandie asked as she made her way around one last couch. Her hair was beginning to come loose from its bun.

"Yeah," Mike said. "Fine. Got a job offer from one Jen Stratford. She's got a place out on the west side of Loop Four-ten."

"Great! I've got four more in my pocket. Business cards, I mean. But damn, I mean, everybody was coming to talk to me about it, like I wanted, and then she went over to John instead... I was sort of planning to tell them about him being special one at a time, you know? Didn't want to yell it out to everyone..."

"It's not a problem, I don't think," Nacho said, coming up behind Sandie. "Weird people get hired all the time. Take Sandie, for example." He winked and grinned. "Only real problem is the legal, but since you did go to the cops... You did, right?"

"Yeah. Almost got in trouble for waiting so long, but apparently it's pretty common for people to not know what to do about finding someone. Everyone knows what to do when you lose someone, but when someone shows up on your back porch... You know? Anyway, they said he can stay with me until they get some results back."

Connie and Mike exchanged a look behind Nacho's back. Neither of them thought it likely that the police would dig up anything of consequence. Still, Mike found himself irrationally hoping for a mundane solution to this whole thing.

Another job offer strode up and presented itself. Connie went off with her new beau, and Mike finished the dregs of his cold coffee. The Zonc slowly emptied.

"I'd call that a success," Nacho said. "That's what, six business cards and a phone number? Not bad at all. And you know, even though my regs don't tip much, you guys are always welcome here. Both of you. We still do slams."

"I'll think about it," Sandie said. "I still don't have a whole lot of extra time, and if I'm driving him around to stuff..."

"Yeah. I get that."

John looked at Mike's shoes. "I..." he said slowly, uncertainly, "...do not want to sing for Jen Stratford."

No one else seemed to have heard. Mike looked at Sandie and Nacho, but they just kept talking. Then he looked at John, who continued his minute inspection of the floor.

"What?" he asked stupidly.

"I do not want to sing for Jen Stratford," John said again. "She..." He trailed off and blinked once, slowly. "She thinks I'm small." He looked up and tilted his head, birdlike.

"You can talk?"

"Yes."

"Since when?"

"Now."

"You just learned how to talk?"

"Yes."

"How long have you been able to understand?"

"Now."

"You just figured out how to understand and talk. Just now."

"Yes."

"Wow."

John blinked. "Yes," he said.

"How?"

"I listened."

"Well, good. That's good. That'll make things a lot easier."

John looked at the ceiling instead of answering. Mike reached over and tugged on Sandie's sleeve.

"You want to pay some attention?" he asked. "There's a breakthrough going on over here."

Sandie turned around with a roll of her eyes, hands on her hips. "Well, good," she said. "What's going on?"

John turned away and spoke to the bar. "I don't want to sing for Jen Stratford."

Sandie blinked. "What?" she asked. One hand slipped off of her hip.

"I don't want to sing for Jen Stratford," John repeated.

Mike laughed.

SEVENTEEN

Bird wings, Sandie scribbled on a yellow legal pad.

Something like flying
Something like burning
When the sky slips away and leaves
Only blue stars.
Each one has a voice. Nebula magic.

John twanged quietly on his guitar, but Sandie could feel him listening in on her creative process. He could have talked if he wanted to, but he did not. *inefficient,* he told her. He talked to Mike, and he talked to Connie, and he talked to Nacho, but talking aloud to Sandie was pointless when she could know/sense/understand/hear him just fine.

words make feelings, he observed. *same-different like music. how?*

Sandie tucked her pen behind her ear. "They just do," she said. "They make you think about things that make you feel. How do you do it?"

dots little dots moving combining moving. tiny song everything song.

"Chemistry?"

He took a moment to think about the meaning he felt in her mind, then nodded. "Chemistry," he echoed. He showed her the little dots moving and combining inside a human brain, then the shallow echo that he skimmed off the top and kept for himself, hoarding droplets of joy to feed on until the next time.

"Dying of apathy," Mike had said as he took her arm just outside the Zone. "I can't imagine stumbling through life without being able to feel it. Can anyone really blame him for wanting that?"

"So he doesn't freak you out anymore?" she asked.

Mike frowned. "I think I understand him better. But he's got a really remarkable ability, something I personally would call supernatural, at least until I know more about it. Either way, it's just a powerful tool, and a tool is only as helpful or harmful as the person holding it. That gift of his could do some serious damage if he uses it wrong - say, if he stops caring how he gets that kick he's looking for."

"He won't," she said, but Mike had a point. Sandie

had a window straight into John's mind, and she could not see anything there that was reckless or controlling or greedy; still, the window was small, and even though she had already figured out that there was nothing she could hide from John, she really had no way of knowing what he might be hiding from her. There was a strange vastness about him, a sense of powerful enormity that did not quite mesh with the curious, damaged, naïve little vagrant she thought she knew. Even if he was exactly what he seemed to be, Sandie had to admit to a little bit of anxiety about what he might become if he ever managed to fix himself. Whatever he really was, it was huge.

"Inefficient," John said softly, drawing a minor chord from the guitar.

Sandie looked up and blinked. "Sorry?"

"Ruling the world. More out than in. Too much... What? Deficit?" He met her gaze and showed her his calculations, including a lightning-quick scenario in which he took over the planet and spent so much energy trying to keep it that he slowly withered away. There was no humor in that thought, or fear, just a frank analysis.

Sandie felt a slow flush creeping up her neck. "I don't think you actually would," she clarified. "It's just that people get scared of things that are different. It's because they don't want to get hurt."

i hurt?

"No, but they don't know that."

you are not scared.

"No. A little worried" – there was no reason not to admit that; he would know whether she said it or not – "but not scared."

i would not hurt. no benefit no sense no logic. maladaptive.

Sandie smiled. "I know, right? There are a whole lot of people who could stand to figure that out.

"Are you ready to go?"

not Jen Stratford.

"Mag's Bar. Mag said her granddaughter's got Asperger's, so she knows about people who are different. She won't treat you like you're small."

John nodded and zipped his guitar into its case, watching the back door instead of his hands. He hummed, and the yard distorted as the glass rippled. He watched the porch a moment longer before turning and making his way to the garage.

no others, he offered by way of explanation.

Sandie imagined a flock of zombies appearing on her back porch, humming in harmony.

"No," she said. "Not yet, anyway."

Mag was a scrawny old woman with spiky grey hair, an ex-biker chick in leather pants with a screaming eagle tattooed across the back of her neck and "Captain Dave ~ Gone but Not Forgotten" wrapped around her right bicep. She wore a powder-blue tee shirt emblazoned with a big, white daisy, seemingly for no reason other than to provide a glaring contrast to the rest of her. Steely blue eyes gave John a critical once-over, and she reached out abruptly to pop the top button of his shirt.

"Loosen up, kid," she croaked. "You'll make folks nervous, roboting around like that. Look, I gotcha all set up over here. Chair, water, got a little fan you can set up if you need. You get hungry, I'll spot you a basket of fries. Anything else you need, just grab me or Kirsten or Andy ~ anybody wearin' a daisy, see? You can go ahead and warm up or whatever you need to do. We open for dinner at five, that gives you 'bout twenty minutes. Happy hour's at seven." She shoved a hand through her spiky hair and wiped it on the front of her shirt, leaving some dry gel behind. The back door slammed, and someone yelled a muffled greeting from the kitchen.

"Should be just about it," Mag said. "Good to have you here, Johnny-boy."

John made a perfunctory attempt at a smile, which Sandie found unspeakably creepy. It was all in the specifics, she thought: the way his lips stretched instead of curved, eyes squinted instead of crinkled.

Mag seemed to appreciate the gesture, though; she reciprocated with a fond left hook to his upper arm.

"Good on you," she growled, showing five gold teeth. "Let's see that smile more often."

"We'll work on it," Sandie whispered as Mag showed her eagle and stumped away. "And try not to knock any socks off, okay? Remember like we practiced?"

He agreed silently, taking up his spot in the chair and unpacking his guitar. The air moved around him, and the blades of the little fan stirred.

Sandie took a seat in a booth nearby. The place had no wifi, but she took out her laptop all the same and updated her spreadsheet of magazine submissions. Four more rejections, one acceptance, two that had yet to get back to her. The acceptance was from *Lead Soldiers*, naturally. They had sent her fifteen dollars and a contributor copy.

Nacho showed up at seven. He seemed to have picked up some preconceptions somewhere, along with contact lenses and a Too High String Band tee shirt.

"Came to check up on the Sound," he said as he sat down. They each had fried catfish, fried okra, and a bowl of chili with beans. They split a pitcher of beer.

"That's not the Sound," Nacho said over his second refill. "Did something happen? That's not... That's not the way it was."

"He's in business mode," Sandie explained. "Everybody was so impressed with what he did at the

Zone, but it occurred to me that spilled drinks and uneaten meals might not go over so well. I mean, it's a bar, you know? He's supposed to be accompanying the usual routine, not knocking it out."

"Good point," Nacho said. He leaned forward to dig his wallet out of his back pocket, fished a card out of the interior, and slid it across the table.

"That's a friend of mine," he said, smoothing his moustache with a fingernail. "He's been looking for the sound, too. I don't know if that'll fly with the cops, or if you're even interested in messing with it, but he can fix things up for you. A bunch of his have performed in the Alamodome. He's worked national tours for a couple. Dozens of big record contracts. If you were looking to, say, rack up some big bucks, dig up some top-notch scientists, get your guy some help and maybe get his face around, see if anyone knows him..."

"Have you been talking to Connie?"

"The one with the hair? No, I just thought... Look, this kind of gig is going to hold him back. You can tell that just by looking. Music is his thing, and he definitely has the potential to make it big. Huge, even. If he's good with playing bars and bingo halls, that's fine. He just needs to know that he could go further if he wanted to."

Sandie bit her lip and picked up the card but did not look at it. She wanted to explain – really, she did – but to an ex? Mike was one thing; best friends do not rat on you, especially best friends with a white collar and an overdeveloped sense of morality. Connie never stopped talking, but she also never said anything she should not. Starving poets were an entirely different ball of wax.

"I don't want him in the public eye," she said. "I'll talk to him, but I really think it's a bad idea. You know there will be someone waiting right there to take advantage of him at every moment. What if he can't handle that? He can barely take care of himself just with the everyday stuff. What about like, navigating airports and signing contracts and messing with crazy fans? Even if he could make it big, that's a lot to handle for anyone, much less someone who can't tie his shoes."

She stuffed her mouth with fried okra before she could say anything she would regret.

John slid into the seat beside her, bearing a basket of french-fries. "A person said I should eat these," he said with a touch of perplexity.

Sandie stuffed the agent's card into her pocket and looked around; said person was a be-daisied employee, an enormous dark-skinned woman practically dripping kitchen grease.

"Kirsten," she said by way of introduction. "Babydoll, you had better keep coming around here, 'cause I am going to put some meat on those bones." She slapped down a bottle of ketchup and moved on to the next table.

Nacho's face twitched. "You heard her, Babydoll," he said seriously. "Eat your fries."

John blinked rapidly.

Sandie fingered the card in her pocket.

EIGHTEEN

John played Mag's Bar and Grill on Wednesdays and Fridays; on Tuesdays, he provided ambience for The Staghorn, a fine-dining establishment that specialized in farm-raised venison; Thursday saw him at Three Rivers Wine Lounge. Saturday night, though, at five-thirty, Mike took over.

"I really kind of don't like this," he told Sandie uncertainly, poking his head out of the vestry with a flash of Ordinary Time green. "We're worshiping. That's not to be used for whatever he's using it for. I mean, it's great if he wants to sing in church, but the whole point is to make a joyful noise *unto the Lord*, and I'm not really sure he gets that concept."

Sandie shrugged and looked at John for help, but John was more interested in the large church calendar pinned to the wall.

"I think he wants a demonstration," she said, raising her voice as Mike disappeared back into the glorified closet to look for a stole. "I was trying to explain faith, and it... sort of didn't work."

"Well, he can sit in, of course. You can help him follow along. Have you even been in since we changed over to the new missal?"

"Yeah." Sandie paused, shuffled, and cleared her throat. "A couple of times."

Mike poked his head back out and grinned. "We'll just call that your confession, shall we?"

"Oh, crap. What's my penance?"

"You're babysitting a singing zombie. I think you're covered for now. But look, I've really got to get a move on."

Sandie hauled John up the stairs to the choir loft, down the stairs to the vestibule, and through the glass doors into the nave.

"Don't make a scene," she whispered as she pushed him into a pew, folded the kneeler down, and shoved her purse under the seat. "Don't say anything, don't sing anything, just do what I do, okay?"

He nodded, glanced at Sandie, and laced his fingers in his lap.

why? he asked silently.

"Just because," Sandie whispered back.

The choir overhead erupted in a blast of soprano and pipe organ, and the procession began. Sandie scrambled to her feet in time to catch a glimpse of Mike – *Father Mike* – and a deacon she did not know, surrounded by four boys who looked less than happy to be wearing black dresses. The one in front, the one bearing the crucifix, had on wheelie shoes, which actually created a startlingly otherworldly effect as the cross glided smoothly down the aisle. Mike flowed serenely along behind, billowing in green linen.

Sandie seemed to remember something about the priest kissing the altar, but it was impossible to see anything around the enormous family of redheads in front of her.

"In the name of the Father," she heard, seemingly from every direction at once, "and of the Son, and of the Holy Spirit!" She turned around and noticed speakers mounted at the base of every other window.

"Amen," she muttered with the rest of the congregation. John gave her a strange look.

"The grace of our Lord Jesus Christ, and the love of God, and the communion of the Holy Spirit be with you all!"

"And also with you," Sandie muttered, while everyone else chorused "And with your spirit."

She bit her lip and fumbled in the back of the pew

for a copy of the missalette, where she hoped an accurate script was to be found. John stood perfectly still, facing straight forward, not looking at anything in particular. She wondered whether he was listening to Mike or to something else, possibly to something only he could hear. She held him back when it was time for Communion, like she knew she was supposed to. He did not argue, but he did tilt his head and watch a dust bunny skitter around the floor, pushed by the struggling air conditioner.

some not all some feel much holding much other-self, he observed.

"Yeah, probably," Sandie whispered under the overpowering strains of the organ. "For them, they're with their God. It's what I was trying to tell you, about believing something you can't prove."

He nodded and closed himself off, thinking about something he did not want her to see. Sandie made a conscious decision not to be worried about that.

"Go in peace," the deacon said, "glorifying God in your life!"

The organ started again, and a redheaded toddler in the next row up began to cry. The congregation filed out after the recessional hymn, but Sandie stayed put, and John stayed beside her. He did not speak or move or even hum along with the last strains of the organ, and he stayed closed off. Sandie wondered whether taking him to church had been a bad idea, even though he had asked her to.

"You okay?" she asked, not bothering to lower her voice too much once the church had emptied.

The Lady of Sorrows, ensconced in her little alcove to one side of the altar, watched with the air of someone trying very hard to be reassuring. The paint on her feet was starting to flake from years of spilled bud vases.

John ignored them both. He looked up at the enormous crucifix above the altar, but the visual symbolism seemed lost on him – or perhaps he understood it perfectly – because it did not hold his attention long. He glanced at the altar servers scurrying along, divested now of their cassocks and seeming much happier. One of them skidded past on wheelie shoes until he collided with a hoary old Knight of Columbus, identified by an old and tarnished lapel pin affixed to his jacket.

"Jackson Parker Bloom, where is your mother?" the Knight growled, and the altar servers scattered.

Mike approached quietly from the side aisle. He was still in his vestments, and there was grayish old-lady lipstick smeared across his jaw.

"You, uh... You've got something kind of... there," Sandie said, pointing.

He swiped at the smudge with the heel of his hand and leaned against the back of the next pew up.

"Everything okay over here?" he asked.

"Pretty good," Sandie said, even though John's silence still worried her. "I think we got a few things figured out. Answered some questions, anyway. Maybe."

Mike looked at John, who was looking at a young man at the front of the church. The young man held a sleeping infant, and he knelt in front of the statue of the Virgin. His shoulders shook. John blinked and squinted.

"I have faith," he said flatly, never once looking away from the young man.

Mike's eyebrows soared into his hairline and he glanced at Sandie. Sandie shrugged and shook her head.

"Um," Mike said. "You do?" He shot a glance at the young man in front of the church, then turned his attention back to John. Sandie could see intense skepticism and professional compassion battling in his expression.

"He thinks someone is there," John said, even more detached than before, "where the rock is. He thinks it will help him." He ran his thumb across the pages of the missalette and turned blank, black eyes on Mike. "That is faith, isn't it? I have some, I think."

Mike had gone just a little bit red, by that point, but he still managed a polite tone. "In what?"

John folded his hands as though in prayer, just like the hurting man who prayed in front of a rock. "Others," he said simply. "I don't know them, but," – and there he paused for a moment, tilting his head to one side like he was listening hard, or perhaps trying to convince himself – "I think I am not alone."

Sandie released a whistling breath and tugged on her ponytail. "Um," she said.

"Oh, geez," Mike whispered. "I bet you're right, and there are others, but even if there aren't, you're not alone. Okay? You've got Sandie. You've got me, if you need me, I guess. And Connie, and, uh, what's-his-name..."

"Nacho," Sandie supplied.

"Yeah, Nacho. You're not alone." Mike joined them on the pew, put his arm around the silent creature, and gave it a squeeze. "Just don't go crazy on us or anything, okay?"

John thrummed.

NINETEEN

The email was unexpected and frankly startling.

Sandie, your dad and I are back in Moscow and we have internet. No phone yet so don't call us we'll call you when we're able. Just letting you know we are going to be back home for Christmas make sure the house is clean okay? If you let any friends move in make them go away unless its Ignacio have you married him yet? When we get home I will make borscht.

Also, call the accountants make sure there is still enough for property taxes things did not go so well so we might have to find a smaller house. No worries not for a while though.

Love your mom.

Sandie regarded the computer screen first without feeling, then with a vague and nameless irritation.

"Great," she said aloud, and she left the computer right there while she drove John to the Staghorn.

The owners of the Staghorn were not nearly as social as Mag, but they were interesting in their own way. Kelly and Kelli McMasters did not believe in allowing a tip jar to mar the tidy ambience of their establishment, but they did pay handsomely for John on Tuesday nights, and they were more than happy to give away samples of exotic jerky. Sandie tried their venison and politely refused their ostrich, emu, water buffalo, and zebra. At their request, John had started to add some classic blues to his repertoire.

He unloaded, unpacked, and set himself up in the niche provided for his performances.

"Where's Kelli?" Sandie asked Kelly, who was supervising his restaurant with the air of a proud parent.

"Out on the ranch," he replied. "We've got a truck full of nilgai to get settled in the back pasture. Bow hunters will pay loads to take one of those. I'm not sure about cooking them ourselves, though. Butchering something that big has got to be a pain."

Sandie made what she hoped was a politely interested noise and backed away from the discussion of butchering. She stayed a while longer, but John did not seem to be having any trouble, so after about an hour, she left her cell phone number on an order pad and went back home.

The computer's waiting reply screen taunted her the moment she walked back inside.

"Aren't you supposed to hibernate or something?" she demanded. The computer said nothing, and she realized that she had become used to talking to things that did not talk back.

Mom, she typed in the box, but nothing else came to mind. She deleted it and started over.

Mom,

I took a guy in, and I can't make him leave. He doesn't have anywhere else to go. He's really amazing, but you'll just have to meet him when you come home. I'll tell you more when you have a phone.

Also, I got another poem in a magazine.

Sandie

She thought for a moment, then added *Love* in front of her name. Then she deleted the whole thing again.

Mom,

I have a friend living here who doesn't have anywhere else to go, and I'm not going to just make him leave. He's really amazing, and I can't wait for you to meet him. I'll see you when you get home. Do I have to pick you up at the airport?

Also, I got another poem in a magazine.

Love, Sandie.

That sounded better, in her opinion, and it lacked the creepy overtones of *I can't make him leave*. It also took out the possibility of discussing the situation, which could only have ended in trouble. And she very deliberately neglected to ask what, exactly, had not gone so well.

I'm not a kid, she added. *I'm holding down the fort for you because you begged me to come back home even though I had my own place, and a sticky note on the fridge is NOT enough warning when you leave the country while I'm at work and expect me to take care of your house for you for a year with nothing but once-a-month emails to let me know you're not in a Pakistani prison or something...*

She deleted that as well, sent the email and watched the screen for a few minutes in case of a delivery error, but the message went through without complication, leaving Sandie with mixed feelings.

She vacuumed until it was time to pick John up and did not respond to his steady, curious stare during the car ride home. He, for his part, did not suck the problem out of her brain, which Sandie decided to take as a sign of improving social skills.

A few fat drops of rain slapped the windshield as they pulled into the driveway. The sight of the house and the thought of the computer waiting inside tightened Sandie's stomach and made her jaw ache, and John's flat black stare intensified. She felt him close himself off; her feelings were just as unpleasant to him as they were to her.

"Sorry," she muttered, throwing the car into park

with a bit more vehemence than necessary.

They managed to get John's instrument inside before the rain began in earnest.

He set up at the kitchen table with a spread of sheet music and Sandie's old mp3 player, bent on figuring out the connection between the marks on the paper and the vibrations in the air.

Sandie started a virus scan on her computer and left it alone to go watch him. He did not seem to mind the way some people would. In fact, he barely seemed to notice her.

"Do you have parents?" she asked after a while, speaking over the drumming of the rain on the kitchen windows.

He rolled the word over in his mind, then searched for meaning in hers.

parents. don't know.

"You know, the people who put you here. The ones who made you."

He reached back as far as he was able, into the cacophony and the fire and the pain. Sandie winced on his behalf.

don't know nothing before no generation origin unknown.

"Sorry," she said again.

He tilted his head to one side as though listening,

then went back to his study of musical notation, apparently unaffected by the horror of his recent past.

"What about home?" she tried after a few minutes of silence. "I mean, I know you can't remember, but you can probably take some guesses. Like, if something here seems strange, then you at least know that where you're from isn't like that."

all strange nothing familiar. different everything or blank all blank.

"You can't have lost everything. There's got to be something left. Some kind of second nature or something."

if so unknown.

She gave up then and went upstairs to shower and try to sleep, but her thoughts turned first to fire and noise and then to the business card sitting in the top drawer of her bedside table. It probably would be good for him, she had to admit. There would be money, surely enough money for the right kind of research, for finding a scientist they could trust to help and not to make John into a guinea pig. They could find someone to figure out what he was and where he belonged, and maybe even how to get him back there. And as a music legend's assistant or agent or whatever, there might even be enough money to get her back out of her parents' house.

She could travel. They could both travel together and

find out whether something like John had ever happened before.

But if they got John back where he belonged...

Sandie was almost starting to hope that never happened. It was like imagining Mike being sent away, but worse, because the worst the Church could do was send him to tend a different flock. There was no telling where John might end up, if his home was someplace Sandie could even imagine.

She fell asleep with that thought in her head and dreamed about crashing through the walls of reality.

TWENTY

The regulars at the JoeHaus had already become accustomed to John by the time the weather began to change and Sandie finally broke out a denim jacket. The sign on the Baptist church down the street still flashed "Pray For Rain," but the grass on the sides of the highway was no longer spontaneously bursting into flame every few days, and the sound of fire truck sirens became a slightly rarer occurrence. The cedars turned brown and shot their pollen into the air like so many allergy-inducing smoke bombs, and all of San Antonio was covered in a thick pall of brown cedar dust until the prayed-for rain finally washed it away.

John commandeered Sandie's laptop, spent two hundred hours on the internet, and came away with a working knowledge of the written word and a lackluster understanding of fashion. He bought five black button-down shirts, five pairs of blue jeans, and a pair of Converse All-Stars. He gave the rest of his earnings to Sandie, and she bought lunch meat and root beer.

And he deteriorated.

It was difficult to see at first. Sandie had watched an aunt die of cancer, once, and that was obvious. There was pain in her eyes and in the lines at the corners of her mouth. She slept and ate and slept, and then she stopped eating and slept all the time. There was the chemo and vomiting, dark smudges under her eyes, sometimes nosebleeds, and crying when she thought everyone else was asleep. There was morphine, tests, biopsies, and finally the steady beep of the heart monitor and the understanding that, sometime soon, the beeping would stop.

John ate macaroni and drank root beer. He probably slept sometimes, though Sandie never saw him at it. He sang as beautifully as he ever had, and he periodically moved Sandie to tears, even though she told him every time to stop doing that. He practiced his guitar and learned to play Greensleeves and Ghost Riders in the Sky. He never let Sandie make him late for work, and he never let her be late for church, which Mike found hilarious and Sandie found obnoxious.

"She will be more efficient with faith," John told Mike while Sandie scowled. "It motivates."

"Faith in what?" Mike wanted to know. Sandie knew

that it was hard for him to keep his sense of humor when it came to religion, but he certainly tried. "You believe in God, now?"

"Not in what," John clarified. "Faith in faith. Otherwise she lies down and doesn't move."

Mike snorted into his coffee and almost choked. "I think you mean hope," he said, and he turned to Sandie. "And you need to be a better role model, lazybones."

John went with her most days to the JoeHaus and watched the customers. A few stopped coming, but more seemed to adopt him as their mascot.

Connie made a poster and hung it on the wall above his habitual table. It read "AWESOME People Only" in six-inch-high orange letters.

But the days grew shorter, and Sandie kept walking into the living room to find her permanent guest staring intently into the darkening back yard.

"Not yet?" she asked every time, and every time he would shake his head.

not yet.

Near the middle of October, she came home after a late shift and found him in the armchair, the same seat Mike had taken when she told him she thought she was possessed. He had his guitar in his lap and a chord sheet on the coffee table, but he was watching the glass door with fervent intensity. Sometimes, she thought he forgot to breathe.

"Not yet?" she asked, dropping her purse onto the table. Pens cascaded across the floor.

He blinked once, flat black eyes flickering from the door to Sandie and immediately back again.

no others.

"Well, no others yet. Maybe someday."

no others.

The next time she asked, he did not answer at all, shut himself off from her, and she wondered whether it might be cruel of her to keep bringing it up. He could not be hurt, she knew, or disappointed, or sad, but there had to be *some* feeling involved in a crisis of faith.

"You shouldn't stop watching," she told him, "just in case. It would really suck if others came and then left because you didn't answer."

He did not stop, but Sandie did not ask anymore.

The business card in the top drawer of her bedside table occupied her thoughts often, but she did not take it out. More often than not, she let the answering machine pick up when Nacho called, even though he rarely asked after John.

John played Our Lady of the Hills Halloween Carnival. Sandie dressed him up in gold lamé, and the general consensus among the throbbing horde of candy-fuelled children was that he was a space alien rock star.

One little girl worked up the courage to represent humanity.

She pulled up one striped stocking and tugged nervously at the tip of her pointed hat as she approached the pumpkin-covered plywood stage.

"You sing pretty," she said, careful to keep one of the amps between herself and the object of her compliment, then added the quick amendment, "even if you're bald."

John took a swig from his bottle of water and favored the girl with a frank stare. "You're not bald," he observed.

"No," she agreed. "I'm not. When it's not in a ponytail, my hair goes almost to my butt. I want to keep growing it until it's to the floor like Rapunzel, but Mom says it would get dirty."

John nodded. "I don't have any hair to grow."

The girl pursed her lips and squinted. "I guess that's okay," she conceded. "You don't have to wash it, and it doesn't pull when you brush it. Only, usually it's really old people who are bald. And people with motorcycles."

"I don't think I'm old," John said. "And I can't drive a motorcycle."

The girl shrugged as though to say there was nothing she could do about that. She fidgeted with her pocket and dropped a folded dollar bill into the tip jar. "That's 'cause Mom said you gave her goosebumps," she said. "That's a good thing. They were good goosebumps."

She hiked up her patchwork skirt and hightailed it across the parking lot, weaving between her awestruck peers. Her courage was astounding.

John sipped again at his water as he watched her go. The sound of voices picked up in the momentary silence.

Sandie looked up from the face painting booth, halfway through transforming a little boy into a rabbit. John met her gaze and understood, launching at once into the next piece.

Evening fell. Children were wrangled and bundled up, and the parking lot emptied.

difficult, John told Sandie as he packed his guitar and helped wheel the amps back into the school gym. *getting harder not enough. need.*

"We'll figure something out," she promised. "We'll get you a gig – a real performance like the one you did at the Zone, something you can really cut loose with, so you can get what you need."

He nodded, and Sandie felt anticipation at the memory of joy. He wanted to smile again.

"We could ask Monsignor Grigorio if you could do a concert here. Not during Mass, but maybe after. You could learn some hymns, and he might let us put an ad in the weekly bulletin. I bet Mike would help us out with that."

mike helps, was the only reply.

"Is something wrong?" Sandie asked. "I mean, something else?"

John blinked and sifted through her thoughts, looking for the right word. It took him a few moments to find it.

"Tired," he said aloud. "I'm tired."

Sandie grabbed his guitar and piled him into the car to drive him home. He made for the couch and sat silently, staring into the dark through the back window, not bothering for once to practice his music.

"Maybe-" Sandie began, but then she stopped. She set down the guitar and went to check her email.

Sandie, No reservations yet, we'll get back to you.

Mom.

No mention of John, no congratulations for the poem she had published. Sandie closed her browser, shut the laptop, and went upstairs to shower.

John had not moved when she came back down, so she draped a blanket over his shoulders and went to bed.

TWENTY-ONE

In the morning, John still had not moved. Sandie left him where he was and called Mike on the way to work.

"Something's wrong," she told him, and recounted some of what had happened the night before. "He said he's tired," she concluded, "and that what he's getting just isn't enough anymore. I guess that might be partly because of the way he's holding back. I thought maybe if he could just cut loose... Do you think Monsignor would let him have a concert at the church? John's a quick study, he could learn some religious songs or some classical or something. I'm afraid he might..."

She paused, thinking back to their brief discussion of taking over the world. The subject had seemed humorous to her at the time, but the result John had predicted...

"Might?" Mike prompted.

Sandie bit her lip.

"Might fade away," she finished. "I don't think... I mean, to borrow a phrase, I don't think he can live on bread alone. I can make him eat and keep his body going, but the rest of him - the part that's really him - I don't think that part is doing so well, right now."

"I'll see what I can do," Mike promised. "And Sandie? I gotta go now, I've got a christening to do, but... You are still being careful, aren't you?"

"Not as much," Sandie admitted. "But I am keeping an eye on him, and if he starts going funny on me, I swear I won't just sit there. Okay?"

"Okay. Come see me later. Or I'll come see you. Does he work tonight?"

"Not Saturdays. Would you talk to him?"

"Of course. I really have to go, though. Talk to you later."

"Bye."

Sandie hung up and dropped her cell phone into the cup holder.

Brandon was waiting for her behind the counter.

"You're late," he said, his mouth twisting in irritation. "You've been doing this a lot, you know."

"John's not doing well," Sandie said. "And I've done this twice. I'm still on time more often than Connie, and you never fuss at her about it."

"I'm uncontrollable!" Connie called from the back.

"Plus traffic on the Loop was a bitch."

Brandon frowned. "Look," he huffed, "I know you've got responsibilities outside of work. Everyone does. But you've got to start paying more attention to the clock."

"What is with him?" Sandie whispered as she tied on her apron.

Connie rolled her eyes. "He's polishing up his resume. Trying to be more professional. Apparently he's aiming for administration something-or-other with some bank after he finishes his business degree."

"Yeah, well he could stand to cut it out. I don't need him calling me out for actually having a life."

=

It took two weeks for Mike and Sandie to get all the details straight and another two weeks to work out all the scheduling kinks. She knew better than to think any of it would be easy, of course, but the month that elapsed saw John go silent, and it worried her.

He went to work and got paid, but he rarely sang at home anymore, rarely practiced his guitar, and when he did, Sandie felt nothing. That worried her even more.

"You can use me," she told him. "Just for the time being, just until your concert. If you need to. I know I told you not to, but it'd be okay just for the time being.

Okay?"

He nodded his understanding, but did nothing about it.

"I'm serious," Sandie said. "I don't want you fading away on me. Remember how you were when you first got here? I don't want you going back to that. That would absolutely suck."

He sent her an eloquent image of a single droplet falling into an empty bucket.

"Okay," she said. "Okay, okay. I get it."

She drove him to the bluegrass bar and nursed a glass of wine as they sat together, listening, but he was listening to something she could not hear. He closed his eyes, spread his fingers, and pressed his palms flat on the tabletop, face blank and smooth.

Sandie left him alone so he could do his thing. It was a decent night. The band wasn't the best she had ever heard there, but it wasn't too shabby, either. She tapped her foot to the rhythm of the double bass and shot Mike a text.

At Hat Bands. Care to join us?

Sure, he replied. *Be there in 20.*

She sent the same message to Connie and got a similar reply.

When she looked up, John was watching her. Social convention caught up to her uncomfortably.

"You don't mind, do you? If Mike and Connie come?"

He did not respond.

"Are you feeling any better?"

Two tiny droplets falling into an empty bucket.

"But..." Sandie glanced around, frowning. "But it helped before when we were here..." It was a little quieter than before, true, but not by much. The people were loud, and the band was loud, and the tiny, cramped dance floor was packed. People were having a good time, dancing, drinking, shouting back and forth. "What's different?"

A bigger bucket.

"What?"

different me. more me.

"How?"

healing coming-together growing. more now than before.

"More what, exactly?"

more me, John repeated. He tapped one fingertip on the tabletop twice, in time to the music, then stopped.

"Will you be able to hold out another week? Just until the concert?" And would the concert even help? Sandie had to wonder. His performance at the Zone had helped before, but then, so had just sitting at Hat Bands, and if the latter no longer had any effect...

John's eyes twitched in Sandie's direction. He blinked

157

once. No answer.

She had to take that to mean that he didn't know, and that was a worrying thought. She watched as he shut his eyes. There was a sense of effort, of strain, like he was reaching and stretching, grasping for as much as he could get. Spending so much energy trying to get energy seemed a little counterproductive, to her.

Mike arrived and bought a beer before he made his way to their table.

"How's it going?" he called over the racket of the band.

Sandie downed the dregs of her wine and spread her hands helplessly.

He sat, frowning. "Oh. Okay. Is there anything I can do?"

Sandie bit her lip. "Call up as many of your seminary friends as you can get a hold of?"

Mike nodded. "I can do that."

Just a week. They could make it a week, surely.

TWENTY-TWO

Sandie hoped for a full church, even though Mike had warned her that the church was only ever full at Christmas and Easter. Well, then, maybe *almost* full, she had countered. But according to Mike, the church was only ever *almost* full on Palm Sunday and Ash Wednesday, the times when you could go to Mass and *get* something. Something tangible, he amended quickly, rolling his eyes. Something other people could see. If the church didn't even fill up when there was an opportunity to come away with plant matter, whole or incinerated, why would people come thronging to see an unknown performer?

Even if they had nearly gotten used to seeing John standing eerie and silent in the back pew, none of them knew him, not really. None of them would feel the need to come support him.

But the handful of old ladies, some in mantillas and some bare-headed, was still a disappointment. Sandie watched from behind the organist's bench and wasn't even sure that all of them were there for John. Some of them seemed to be clutching fistfuls of rosary beads, and the ones who actually did seem to be waiting might have actually been adoring the Blessed Sacrament. Sandie wasn't sure. She hadn't been a good Catholic for quite a few years, at least not until John started making her go to Mass regularly, and she was pretty sure that being a good Catholic included more than just an hour a week. She was supposed to go to Confession and stuff. Those little old ladies probably went to Confession and stuff. She watched them closely.

There was still time, though. The concert was scheduled for six o'clock, well after most of the congregation should have gotten off work. If someone else was coming, they still had half an hour to get there. Anyone who had picked up a weekly bulletin or heard the weekly announcements still had time to arrive, if they were going to.

John sat just beyond the organist's bench, behind the tiered choir stand. For a short while, he had seemed more animated, less listless, no doubt picking up on Sandie's enthusiasm, but Sandie was getting nervous, and John was withdrawing again. He studied the statue of the Lady of Sorrows in her alcove to the side of the altar, and

Sandie had no idea what he was thinking. He would not be disappointed if no one else came. He couldn't be. But there had to be something there, even if he wouldn't let her feel it. He was tired. He was hungry. She knew that, even when he had closed himself off. He was empty and hollow, and that made her sad for him. This had to help. It wouldn't be enough, not with so few people. The image of single droplets falling into an empty bucket stuck with her. Plink. Plink. But it had to help some. It had to be enough to hold him until they thought of something better. It had to be enough for the moment, for right now.

Mike bustled around, seeing to the sound system, even though they both knew John didn't need a microphone to be heard clearly in every corner of the church. He was just keeping busy, Sandie knew. He was worried about John. Yes, he was still being careful, urging Sandie to be careful, not to put too much trust in something neither of them could identify, but he still worried. That didn't surprise Sandie too much; worrying was just what Mike did. And besides, he had sort of absorbed John into his flock, regardless of whether a musical pseudo-zombie even *could* be Catholic. Mike was a pretty decent shepherd, despite his insecurities. He couldn't *not* care for someone who needed help.

He caught Sandie's eye and tried for a reassuring smile. It wasn't reassuring, but it was a little goofy, and

Sandie smiled back. Then, as one, they both looked at John. John did not smile. He did not even look back at either one of them. He seemed lost in thought, focused hard on something inside himself. Or maybe resting, Sandie thought. She had still never seen him sleep. Maybe he didn't sleep, just spaced out and disengaged from the world around him. In a world where everything was miserably strange, paying attention, processing, had to become exhausting after a while.

She looked back at Mike, shrugged, and shook her head. Mike wandered back into the vestry.

Connie was nowhere to be seen. She had said she would come, but Connie was distractible, and Sandie couldn't be too terribly mad at her. She had probably seen something shiny and wandered off somewhere between her place and the church. Come to think of it, Connie might not have been too comfortable in a church, anyway. Sandie thought of her necklace with its cluster of religious medals, but she was pretty sure that one of those medals depicted Santa Muerte, Saint Death, who wasn't popular with Mike's sort of Catholic.

Connie was nowhere to be seen, but Nacho had slipped in and taken a seat in the very back, smooth and cool once more in his black linen jacket and dark jeans. Sandie wasn't sure how he had even heard about the concert, and she was momentarily annoyed – even more annoyed when he grinned and winked at her, showing no sign that he was mad at her for screening his calls – but she made herself remember why any of them were there. They were there for John, and every little bit, even Nacho, helped.

Quarter of an hour left.

Sandie got up and went to sit next to John. She took his hand and squeezed, even though she knew gestures weren't what he needed. It made her feel better, and maybe if he was picking up on her feelings, it would make him feel better, too. Just a little bit.

He didn't move, but she could feel his attention on her. He was waiting for her to say something, but she had nothing to say.

Ten minutes.

Five minutes.

Four.

Three.

Staring at her watch, Sandie felt she should be bored, but every second that ticked by only heightened the tension. This had to work. It had to help him.

Two.

Sandie nudged John to his feet and handed him his guitar. For a moment, he only stood there, and she worried that he wasn't even going to be able to muster the will to play, but he shuffled toward the microphone in front of the organ. His fingers twitched on the frets.

Sandie breathed out and moved forward as well, sliding in front of him to address the tiny assembly. Two more people slid in through the door and joined Nacho in the furthest pew. One of them had a disconcertingly professional air about him, and Sandie wondered whether it was that agent. That might explain Nacho's smug nonchalance. Maybe he thought he was getting back at her for not calling him, going over her head... No, that was just paranoia. She swallowed the thought and wondered where that kind of negativity could have come from. Nacho wasn't a vindictive person. Never had been. There was no reason for her to be suspicious of him.

She cleared her throat.

"Um," she muttered into the microphone. "Hi. Thank you all for coming." What else did one say at a concert in a church? It wasn't the same as when John had sung at the Zone. These were old people, some of whom looked startled at the interruption. It wasn't even a concert, was it? More like a recital. The ones who had even known about it were there to hear hymns, not to hear John or any other particular person sing them. Best to keep it short, then.

"We've put together a short set, just some classics and some old favorites. So, um, without further ado... John Doe!"

There was a ripple of whispering at the odd name, but no applause. Okay, then.

Sandie stepped back and motioned John forward. He looked at her expressionlessly. There was a question behind his blank face. What if it doesn't help? He couldn't be afraid of that possibility, couldn't be anxious or nervous, but the thought was there, and Sandie didn't have an answer.

Just sing, she told him silently, trying to fill the thought with as much reassurance as she could. *Won't know until we try. And if it doesn't work, we'll figure something else out. Just sing.*

His head moved just a fraction, like a nod. He shifted his guitar and stepped up to the microphone.

Sandie knew what came next, and she hurried back to her seat. She didn't want to find out what would happen if she was standing when he started.

And, horrifically, for a moment, nothing did happen.

His fingers pulled a beautiful, baroque intro from the guitar, and after a few bars, he opened his mouth and began an inhumanly lovely Our Father. He sang like an angel.

But that was all it was. A song, gorgeous, but nothing more.

There was a murmur of approval from some of the audience, a few old women who had lost the ability to whisper. They loved it. But they weren't blown away. They weren't lost in it.

Sandie caught her breath and looked around. Mike had appeared behind the organ bench, frowning. He glanced at her, eyebrows pulling down, and she shook her head helplessly. Nacho had leaned over to whisper into the professional man's ear.

It had gone wrong. All that planning, all that hoping, and it had gone wrong after all. John was too tired even to get what he needed.

Then she was calm again. Her panic siphoned away and was gone. It wasn't much. Even as badly freaked out as she was, she was still just one drop in a growing bucket. But it was enough. Her panic siphoned away, and the song began to change.

It was subtle, at first. A little, quiet ripple that she almost didn't notice. A little leap, like a kite catching a light breeze, not enough to make it fly, but enough for an instant of lift. So gentle that even when she did notice it, she almost didn't recognize it.

A little leap, a little skip.

Sandie relaxed and glanced toward Mike. It wasn't quite okay just yet, but it still could be. John might still be able to do it.

And then the Our Father unfurled like wings, and Sandie had time to wonder whether, this time, she might be used to it enough that she could actually pay attention, figure out what it was that made that sound so special...

Half an hour later, John paused for breath, and Sandie realized that, no, she probably wouldn't ever be so used to it that it didn't blow her away. She swallowed hard and shivered, nodding in agreement with something no one had said.

John leafed through his sheet music, probably just for show. It only took him moments to memorize a piece of music, but she had told him to pretend, to be as human as possible, and so he pretended that he needed to find the next piece.

Slowly, the sound of voices returned as the little old ladies, one by one, remembered how to think. A few dabbed lacy hankies at their cheeks. A few asked each other what that last song had been, but no one seemed able to remember. No one seemed concerned about that fact, either.

John's eyes seemed a little brighter. The buzz of his thoughts in the back of Sandie's mind seemed a little louder, a little stronger. He did not smile, but maybe after the second set...

He glanced up at her, sensing the speculation, and nodded almost imperceptibly.

better stronger not enough not enough but not gone yet.

He showed her himself, fading, but very slowly. It would hold him until they found something more, but it was barely enough to keep him alive, and not even close to enough to keep him healing.

Not enough, but enough for now. Performance would keep him going.

She shared that realization, and he nodded again, and the next set began, and Sandie was lost again.

TWENTY-THREE

Performance would keep him going. That was a good thing to know, of course. The problem was with finding another venue, something just as big, that would keep him from dying, or even bigger, because just not-dying was no way to live.

Monsignor Grigorio agreed to another concert in a month's time, but only because the first one had gotten good feedback. Mike tried to convince Sandie that they should let Grigorio in on the secret, but Sandie refused.

"He's the Church," she objected. Maybe John made her go to Mass every week, but that didn't mean she trusted the Establishment as far as she could throw it.

"*I'm* the Church, too," Mike pointed out. "And I haven't shipped him off to the secret dungeons that the Vatican totally keeps just in case of alien invasions. Grigorio's a good guy, Sandie. He might be able to help, or know someone who could."

The sarcasm didn't escape Sandie's notice, but she chose to ignore it. "You're not the Church, you're Mike."

"*Father* Mike," he corrected, but he let it go.

A month was too long, though. Sandie couldn't have said how she knew that, but it made sense, and it sounded right. John needed more, and if they couldn't finagle *more*, they could at least finagle *more often*. Another concert at the church would probably be a little more successful. The little old ladies had loved him, and they would tell their little old lady friends, who hopefully would make time to come see what all the fuss was about. But there had to be something for the meantime.

What else, though? Plant him in the middle of Brackenridge Park with a guitar and hope enough passers-by stopped to listen? Take him downtown to play in front of the Alamo? But you had to have a permit for that, didn't you? She was pretty sure you had to have a permit.

Yeah, it had to be a private venue, and something she didn't have to pay for, because she had looked into her parents' finances after all, and it was looking like she would be responsible for the property taxes until they got back. Even with her income and John's put together, that was going to be a challenge. They certainly couldn't afford to rent a hall or anything.

And it killed her that currency was one of the few things he just flat couldn't figure out. She couldn't do the obvious thing that would help him most, and he didn't understand why. That didn't hurt or anger him, but his simple, curious confusion was bad enough.

Only one choice, then.

Sandie called Nacho.

"Hey," she said. "It's me."

The voice on the other end was amused. "Yeah, I know. I have caller ID."

"Oh. Right. So, I was wondering if you have anything booked for tomorrow night."

"Why, are you asking me out?"

She didn't dignify that with an answer. "Can John come sing?"

Nacho took the hint. "Sing like work, or sing like he did the first time?"

For a moment, Sandie held her breath. That question meant that Nacho had identified a difference – a significant difference – between the two. How could he not? But the difference was there, and it was the difference between human singing and... something *else*. Was that what Nacho meant? Did he know that it was something *else*, or did he just think of it as extraordinary?

"Like the first time," Sandie answered.

"Oh!" Nacho made a little pleased noise and clicked his tongue against his teeth. "Great. I'll invite some friends. I mean, he's great all the time, but it's so much better when he's *great* great, y'know?"

"Yeah. Yeah, thanks, Nacho."

"Sure thing. What are you looking for, exactly? Tips? More gigs?"

Oh. Crap. "No, nothing, really. He just wants to come play."

"Oh!" That seemed to please Nacho even more. She could almost hear him nodding vigorously. "That's awesome. I'll say it again: you guys are welcome whenever. You know that."

"Oh, um. Yeah. Thanks. See you around nine?"

"Sure, great. See you then."

She hung up and noticed John watching her. He had been more animated since the evening at Our Lady of the Hills, more engaged, more *there*. He had started practicing again, though not much, and he still stared out the back door, waiting, though Sandie never asked him about others. He had his guitar in his hands, and his fingers moved over the frets as he considered her and her conversation. The strings vibrated a little, humming quietly, even though he was not strumming.

"You're going to play at the Zone after work tomorrow," she said.

He thought about that for a moment. Then he nodded.

"There won't be a whole lot of people there, but it'll still be something."

"Something," he echoed.

And then, to Sandie's surprise, he said, "Great."

Her eyebrows went up. "Are you approving, or just imitating me?"

His black eyes flickered toward Sandie's computer, where he had been planted for quite some time, earlier. The beginning of a thought started to trickle through to Sandie, but it cut off as he decided to try to deliver the information aloud.

"Sarcasm," he explained. "It is saying something to express the opposite."

Well, he was right. There wasn't a whole lot Sandie could say to that, though, somehow, she had never imagined him able to use sarcasm. "Do you not want to sing at the Zone?"

He thought about that, too, then blinked. "It'll still be something," he replied.

"It's all I've got, though. Do you have any other ideas? Something you'd rather try?"

He stared at her steadily, no longer blinking at all, his thoughts silent. There was something, Sandie could tell. Something he was choosing not to share with her. And it was extremely creepy, the way he stared without saying a thing...

will consider keep thinking keep trying.

The thought had a weird feel to it, like there was something else underneath, something Sandie wasn't quite getting. But was it something he wasn't quite sure about, or something he was trying to hide from her? More strangeness. She frowned and looked away, suddenly realizing that he was aware of her doubts. It worried her, and he would know that.

And, worse, this time, he made no attempt to reassure her.

She stood up abruptly and left the room, taking her laptop with her. John did not watch her go, but he had no need to. Of course not. He wasn't really the person-shaped thing she could see. The real John wasn't a John at all, had no eyes any more than it had feelings. She could feel his attention following her, all the same...

"Stop it," she growled to herself, flopping onto her bed. "You're not being fair. Creepy doesn't mean evil. Everyone keeps secrets. I keep secrets. There's nothing wrong with that."

It took her a while to convince herself, though, and a while longer to decide not to say anything to Mike. Mike would understand a momentary freak-out. He wouldn't come swooping in to try to rescue her over one flustered phone call. He would be glad that she still had a cautious side and didn't just place trust blindly. But he would ask what she was going to do about it, and she had no idea what she was going to do about it, and so she did not call.

Nacho was only a few numbers down on her speed dial. She thought about calling him, too. Calling to cancel, because John was clearly not enthusiastic about the prospect, and because if it did help, if it did make him better, he'd be one step closer to being... what? For a moment, he hadn't been John at all, but a creepy white thing with creepy black eyes and inhuman powers and vast, unknowable secrets, and that was terrifying.

She rolled over and pulled out the drawer of her bedside table. The agent's card was still down in the bottom, somewhere. Nacho had mentioned the Alamodome. God, what would happen if John made it someplace like that? He wasn't ready yet – still couldn't figure out how to tie shoes – but even if he did someday become independent enough to handle celebrity, would he just keep growing? What would he turn into?

She slammed the drawer shut and rolled back onto her back. Hell, no. No stadium-sized concerts just yet. Maybe not ever.

And she avoided John for the rest of the evening, even knowing that he didn't have to be in the same room to be in her head. She avoided him the next day, right up to the time she had to drive him to work, and she avoided looking at him in the car.

For his part, John avoided her, too. Her churning cocktail of inner conflict probably tasted bad.

=

Sandie didn't stick around once John was safely dropped off, not this time. She didn't go home either, though, or to the JoeHaus.

She went to Our Lady of the Hills.

She didn't think she had ever been to a church just to go to a church, before. It was always to see Mike, or for a wedding or a funeral or somebody's quinceañera, or because John bugged her about it until she packed him into the car and took him. She wasn't even sure why now seemed like a good time. It just made sense.

The big main doors were locked, so she circled the building to the side door and ducked in there, shuffling up to sit in the very first pew, where she was pretty sure she had never sat before in her life. The Lady of Sorrows stared at her. Sorrowfully. She guessed that only made sense, but it still made her feel like she was doing something wrong.

"I could use a sign or something," she muttered. "Y'know, if you guys still do that kind of thing. It'd be a lot easier to do right if someone would tell me what right is in this, uh, situation."

The statue didn't answer, and she remembered John's

comment about talking to rocks and how hard Mike had tried not to show how much that pissed him off. It had pissed her off, too, Sandie realized. She had never been religious, but she thought she was pretty darned spiritual. She did believe.

Maybe that was why the church felt like the right place to go, because it was something John truly had no part of, no matter how many Sundays he made her go to Mass. He didn't believe in things. He had said he had faith in others, but that was inference, not belief. Others hadn't come, and so he stopped believing. There wasn't love or beauty or joy in his universe, not unless he took it from someone else.

A parasite, Sandie realized suddenly. He never gave anything, only took. His taking didn't hurt anything, as far as Sandie could tell, but could something incapable of giving really be good?

And what about something that was living in a human corpse? That was an aspect she had not considered in a while, but it came back to her now with force.

Sandie groaned and leaned forward to rest her forehead on the rail in front of her.

"Need some serious help, here," she muttered.

A low, gruff voice, very nearby, startled her.

"With what?"

She jerked her head up, making the back of her neck cramp, and saw Monsignor Grigorio standing a short ways away in his too-short cassock and old-man socks. He raised his enormous eyebrows at her and waited.

"Knowing what to do, I guess."

To her surprise, he didn't ask for more specifics or settle in to offer advice. He folded his arms. "Try praying on it."

"'S what I've *been* doing," Sandie groused. She jerked her head toward the statue. "*She* doesn't have much to say on the subject."

Monsignor Grigorio harrumphed. "You know *she* is fiberglass and plaster, right? She doesn't tend to say much, just in general."

Sandie blinked at him, more than a little shocked to hear a priest echo John's thoughts. He must have seen it in her face, because he held his hands up in a peace gesture and came to sit beside her.

"Pagans pray *to* statues," he clarified. "Catholics pray *through* statues. You don't keep a photo on your shelf and think the people in it can hear you when you talk to them. You keep it there to remind you to give them a call. So you don't pray to the statue. The statue is just a reminder."

He paused just long enough for her to begin to think he was done, then continued in a growl. "You'd know that if you'd ever come to Sunday school, Sandie Melindrez.

"And you're doing it wrong, anyway," the old priest concluded.

Sandie blinked at him, but no explanation was forthcoming. "Doing what wrong?"

He looked at her, and his eyebrows seemed to fluff like indignant birds. "Praying wrong."

Okay, Sandie thought. Maybe her theology wasn't exactly up to snuff, but she was pretty sure that she at least knew how to pray. That wasn't that hard. She fluffed up, indignant, herself.

Grigorio ignored her stuttered protest. "The second you sat down," he said, "your lips started moving. And I went to get some stuff done, and when I came back, they were still moving, and they didn't stop until I sat down, which tells me that you're talking too much. Now, if you came and asked me for advice, then didn't stop talking long enough for me to answer, would you get an answer? No. Half of praying is shutting up and listening. Chances are, you already know what to do, but you're not hearing the answer you've got."

There wasn't much Sandie could say to that, as she wasn't sure whether it made sense or not.

Not that it mattered. Time was up, and she had to go pick John up from work and take him to the Zone. Still, she might have gotten in a last question, but the

Monsignor had already hauled himself up and was plodding back the way he had come, stegosaurus-like.

"Well, thanks," she called after him, grabbed her purse, and got up as well.

TWENTY-FOUR

The Zone was packed like Sandie had never seen it before, standing-room only, almost claustrophobic. The fire marshal would have crapped himself to imagine the kind of catastrophe that would result if anything actually did go up in flames. She hoped the drinks were distributed sparingly.

John broke away from her side immediately and made for the cracked linoleum behind the scenes. She let him go. No, he wasn't self-sufficient, but he could probably manage to unpack his instrument, find a prop microphone, and get back out into the lounge without causing any problems. Or any fires. And besides, Sandie still desperately needed time to get her head in order.

She skirted around the edge of the room, looking for an unoccupied seat, even though she was halfway planning to step outside for the duration of the ordeal.

There were no unoccupied seats. In fact, there wasn't even an unoccupied foot of wall space, and she wound up throwing quite a few unintentional elbows, other people's assorted appendages making uncomfortable contact with her ribs, as well.

It was a relief when Connie grabbed her by the shoulder and dragged her into what seemed to be a fort built of plush armchairs and throw pillows. Inside the makeshift Chairhenge, she could begin to breathe.

"Connie! Didn't know you'd be here." She nodded to the other people inside the circle: Connie's dapper beatnik friend – false glasses and fedora, this time – and a pair of tattooed and pierced individuals she thought she recognized from Connie's garage band.

"Tch-*yeah!*" Connie flipped her mohawk back and gave Sandie a look. "Heard there was something going down, and I sure as hell wasn't going to miss it. Can't believe you didn't call me. Don had to tell me." Connie picked at the sheer, silky gloves that covered her arms up to the elbow and nodded at the beatnik. Come to think, it might have been either 'Don' or 'Dawn'; Sandie wasn't sure.

"Whatever," Connie continued. "Pretty good turnout for a last-minute thing. Damn good turnout, actually. Guess word gets around."

Sandie nodded nervously. It was a good thing, she told herself, that word was getting around. John could use everything he could get. Not seventy thousand people crammed into a stadium, or anything, but this was still better than she had expected.

Suddenly, she could feel his eyes on the back of her head, and she turned to find him watching her, expressionless, as the lights condensed around him. Nacho would be manning the electrics somewhere, making that otherworldly glow swirl and flicker to catch everyone's attention before the performance began. It was just theatrics, nothing more, but the ribbons of gold and blue light snaking their way across John's skin made him look as though he was pulsing with energy like a nuclear reactor.

The effect worked like a charm, and the chatter ceased as everyone turned to look.

Nearly everyone. Sandie tried to wriggle back out of the circle of chairs, but Connie caught her by the arm. "What's the matter?"

"Think I forgot to lock the car," Sandie muttered lamely, just as the first vivid chord burst from John's guitar. She realized that she didn't recognize the intro. It wasn't something he had performed before, or something he had been practicing. Was it something he wrote? Could he even write music?

She sat down quickly, knowing that if she didn't, she would get blown away. Something was going to be different, she could tell. At the church, she'd had a few moments to analyze, to witness the thing getting going, but John was in better shape now, and...

How long had that been? An hour? John did seem to favor one hour sets, maybe just for the neatness of the thing. She had an impression of rock and roll, though how that was possible with one vocalist and one acoustic guitar, she wasn't certain. Had he ever sung rock before? Did he even know what it was? Apparently so, because the fading quiver in Sandie's gut had a different feel to it than it had before, something that was just as elated as it had always been, but also a little hard, a little defiant. It tasted like fun, whatever that meant.

She glanced around to measure the effect on everyone else. The eyes around her were wide and bright, pupils dilated, a few chests heaving. Connie and her little posse all wore huge, manic grins. So did many of the other patrons, and this time, nobody seemed to have dropped anything or fallen, even though nearly everyone had been standing when it started.

John caught her attention with a silent call, and she looked over. His eyes were wide and bright, too, the tendons in his neck taught. She could see the pulse throbbing in his temple. He met her gaze, not smiling back at her.

Are you okay?

yes. preferable effective new process. favorable trial. larger scale required.

Sandie bit her lip. A larger scale simply wasn't in the cards, not yet. Maybe not ever, but mostly just not yet. Not until she knew more, understood more, and could make a safe call.

inaccurate. possible probable not dependent on understanding.

"Crap," she muttered, trying again to get up, but a second set began, and there was nothing she could do.

And when she finally blinked and shook herself and looked around, John was gone.

TWENTY-FIVE

Panic seemed like a perfectly reasonable reaction, but there was still chemistry to contend with, and her brain was still flooded with serotonin. She wouldn't be useful until it had passed, and she knew it, so she sat with Connie and her chattering group and kept an eye on the people milling through the room, hoping to recognize a bald head.

What had that been, exactly? Did he contradict her and then intentionally prevent her from arguing? Or was it just something that hadn't even occurred to him? Maybe he'd been intending to start his second set then, and the timing was just unfortunate, but it sure *felt* like he'd shut her up on purpose. Was that because he actually did, or because she was getting paranoid? Either way, he had still contradicted her. He knew there were possibilities she hadn't let him explore, and he meant to explore them.

Finally, she shook herself again and slipped away from Connie, ducking into the back to find Nacho on the off chance that he had seen where John went.

He was there in the dingy linoleum kitchen, sitting at the dingy, cracked table. They were both there, and the professional looking man from Our Lady of the Hills. John blinked at her, maybe trying to look innocent, if he even had a concept of innocence. There was more life in him than she had seen in ages, but if he had managed to soak up any joy, he was keeping it inside. His face remained blank.

"Hey," Nacho said.

Sandie bristled, drawing herself up and getting ready to give him what for, but he continued, "Been waiting for you," and that threw her enough to knock down her bluster.

"Waiting?"

"Yeah, sure. Sandie, this is Humberto Gallegos, my agent friend."

"Bert," said the agent, rising a little from his seat as he reached across the table to shake Sandie's hand.

Sandie shook a little numbly. She was going to have to give Nacho a good talking-to later, but it would just be bad form to explode in front of a stranger. Poor Bert didn't look like he had any idea that he might have crossed a line. For all he knew, he was there by engraved invitation. What good friend wouldn't be thrilled to see the musician sitting across the table from an agent?

And somehow, that thought pissed her off even more, that it was all nice and set up so she couldn't argue. Well, screw that.

"I thought we had already discussed John's career at length," she said sweetly.

Nacho blinked at her, then turned and blinked at John, too. "You didn't talk to her? Should have talked to her, man." He returned his attention to Sandie and shook his head. "He called right after you did. Guess I figured you were standing right there with him, or... No? Oh, well. Sorry."

And just like that, he brushed it off entirely, sat, and got down to brass tacks. Bert Gallegos was outlining commercial possibilities, and John was nodding like he understood, and the three men – two men and a something-else – seemed to have forgotten about Sandie entirely.

She stood there for a while, trying to keep up, but she was at a significant disadvantage. Bert Gallegos knew the industry and was dropping buzzwords and jargon like they were going out of style. Sandie could believe that Nacho had at least some idea what was being discussed, since he and Bert hung out regularly. John could probably just pick the meaning out of their heads or something, or he'd been reading up on the subject behind her back, the same way he had called Nacho behind her back...

And he was watching her, staring steadily past Bert, who was pulling up charts and figures on his phone for the others to look at. His expression was still closed, but she saw confusion in the big black eyes.

i hurt?

That conversation seemed so far away now, when they were getting him ready for his first gig at Mag's Bar, and he had made... not a pledge, but at least a statement. Would not hurt. No benefit no sense no logic. Maladaptive. That was before he had learned how to sneak.

Yeah. Yeah, a little bit. You heard me thinking about the agent.

yes. effective efficient action. greater scale. ...why hurt?

Just would have been nice if you'd talked to me about it, first. This may not be a good idea.

i hurt. i hurt you. speculate will hurt others?

Maybe. Or that others might hurt you. This is going to get really complicated, really quick.

He nodded, and Sandie cleared her throat. Bert cut off mid-sentence and glanced up at her with a smile.

"Um," she started. Speaking was not her strong point, not without something to read from or recite. "So, I've kind of been acting as John's stand-in agent until he's ready to take steps forward, and I think I'd like to talk to my..." – *client* was on the tip of her tongue, but that would sound pompous – "...my friend in private for a few minutes, before this actually turns into negotiations."

"Oh." Burt frowned thoughtfully, then grinned and shrugged. "Yeah, sure. Sorry, I get carried away, sometimes. Tend to go too fast."

Sandie beckoned to John to come with her and started back toward the kitchen door, but he didn't move.

"C'mon," she said. "Wanna hash a few things out, real quick."

But he still didn't move.

effective efficient action. willing to accommodate risk.

"We'll talk later," he said aloud. "I want to hear the rest." And then he lifted a hand and made a shooing motion, dismissing her. "You go. I'll meet you."

And that was that. She was dismissed.

"Um... okay? I'll wait for you."

She waited, not really listening as Connie chattered endlessly, wondering whether she was concerned or overbearing, paranoid or justified, and whether she really had any right to feel hurt. John was right. Going big was probably the fastest way to get him what he needed. Could he handle it, though? He had figured out how to use a phone, which was something, and he had seemed to understand Bert's meandering explanations, so maybe he could learn fast enough to keep up with the demands. Could she, though? Would she have a part in this, once it got rolling? *If* it got rolling?

And there were other concerns, the possibility that someone out there would look at him and see something other than a person with some peculiarities, would hear him and recognize true strangeness, and what then? Would someone try to use him? Would men in black suits show up, and if they did, what would they want? To catch him or study him or destroy him? And would there come a point when he needed to be destroyed? There was more of him now. He was growing as he healed, turning into something she could comprehend even less than before. If he just kept healing, growing into something that even a stadium audience couldn't satisfy, the next step might be a city, a state, the country. There wasn't any reason to think that he would eventually just stop needing more and more. What would that even mean?

Something Mike had said came back to her: "Stumbling through life without being able to feel it." She could almost picture hundreds of thousands of San Antonians wandering around, dying of apathy.

Paranoid or justified?

i will not hurt.

Jesus Christ, will you stay out of my head!

Connie elbowed her in the ribs. "You want to go lie down or something? You're looking... Damn, I don't even *know* what color that is."

Sandie shook her head. "I'm fine. Think I'm allergic to something in here, though. Gonna go sit in the car. See ya later." She took her leave and shuffled out to crouch in the dark parking lot behind locked car doors.

?

She turned the key just far enough to power the electrics and flipped the radio on, filling the car with guitar and trumpets and *gritos*, and ignored the silent question.

?

It was hard to drown out something in your head with sounds from outside. She tried a moment longer before giving up.

What?

why?

You'll have to be more specific.

ugly feel shouting feel like...

There was a pause. He wasn't even using words, and he still couldn't figure out what to say. A sensation rocked Sandie, a brief flash of his first memory, bright and hot and sharp and loud and shattering.

at me. hurting feel. why?

You're listening all the time, aren't you?

yes.

"Oh, God," she muttered, curling up in the seat. Always listening, aware of every thought that went through her. *I'm so sorry. I'm so, so sorry. It's just… people are afraid of things they can't understand. And I can't understand you. I just can't. And I want to say I know you don't mean to hurt me, but you should have talked to me. Now you've gone behind my back, and I can't trust you.*

And she had seen it coming. That was the bad part. She had seen him hiding something, known something was wrong, and tried to rationalize it. Monsignor Grigorio's advice seemed irrelevant, now.

you try to hide from me. secret conceal effective efficient action. want stasis stillness no-healing.

There was a hard edge in that thought, not anger, but close to it. He was juiced up on happiness and didn't quite have the capacity for anger, but it was a solid effort on his part.

Because I'm trying to protect people, including you. I can't just rush into something without having even the tiniest idea what the outcome will be. You shouldn't, either. You're smarter than me, I think. I mean, I know. But you don't know a damned thing about this world and how it works, and you don't seem to know a damned thing about how you work, and you sure as hell don't know a damned thing about how you and it will mix.

protect by hurting? how?

Now that was anger. Her own, she thought, reflected back at her. And he wasn't trying to apologize for hurting her feelings. Maybe he understood her feelings and maybe he didn't, but he absolutely seemed to believe that he was in the right. No, she was hurting him, somehow – by being angry with him? – and he was demanding to know why.

She didn't know. There was nothing she could tell him. It seemed miserably unfair that she wasn't allowed to be angry at him.

Sorry. It's not intentional. I'll try to figure out how to stop.

It didn't matter, though. When John finally did come out, he climbed into Nacho's car and left, and that was that. Sandie cranked up the engine and went home alone. Some time apart seemed like a good idea.

TWENTY-SIX

Typically, if someone was knocking on the door at two in the morning, Mike assumed that it was either police or pranksters. Not that people often knocked at his door at two in the morning; people who needed a priest asap were usually somewhere else and would call to have him meet them.

So he was surprised to see John on the doorstep, glowing weirdly white in the dark. And alone. He peered around, to one side and the other, but Sandie was nowhere in sight. No cops or pranksters either, which was sort of a relief.

"What happened?" he asked nervously as he flipped on the porch light.

The black eyes drifted aimlessly, the way they had at first, before snapping into focus on Mike's face. "You tell people what to do."

For a moment, Mike wasn't sure whether that was a statement about the priesthood in general or if he was being personally accused of bossiness, but John continued, apparently sensing the confusion in the silence.

"When someone takes an action..." He paused, cocking his head to one side as he thought. "When someone takes an action that generates an undesirable outcome, they can tell you, and you tell them what to do."

"You want advice?"

The eyes flickered, huge dark pupils twitching down and then up again. "No... Yes. No. *More.*"

More than advice. Okay. Mike frowned, considering, and then his eyebrows rose. People came to talk to him about their bad decisions all the time. He wasn't sure why that hadn't occurred to him immediately, except that John wasn't really capable of looking contrite.

"You want to confess?"

The eyes locked back onto his face, intense, and something needle-sharp and scalpel-precise stabbed through his mind. He gasped and recoiled, but stepping back did nothing to widen the distance. The probe – *appendage?* – dug around until it discovered meaning, picked apart the concept of sacramental reconciliation, divided it into forgiveness and divine mercy and counseling, investigated each of those individually, and finally withdrew.

"Yes, I want this."

Mike dug the heel of his hand into his eye. The pain wasn't physical, but that was the closest he could get to it. "Ow."

"I hurt?"

"Yeah, you... Ow. What did you do? How did you do that?"

"I didn't know the word. I get my words from Sandie, but she isn't here." There was a beat, the thing on the doorstep watching him, unblinking. "I didn't know it would hurt. You are very small. I can't... I can't see you very well."

That made exactly no sense to Mike, but he was already recovering, and he supposed it was probably the closest he was going to get to an apology, so he let it slide. "Don't do it again, okay? Or at least ask first. That was... I thought you couldn't read other people's minds. Only Sandie's."

"I learned. I'm not good at it."

Mike nodded slowly and finally realized that they were having a conversation in the doorway. He stood aside. "Well, come on in, I guess."

John trailed after him into the dark interior of the rectory, humming quietly. Like sonar, Mike guessed. He knew his own way around his own dark house, but for someone who didn't know the location of every chair and table, it had to be mighty handy to have a way to see without the use of eyes.

Mike flipped a lamp on and sat, gesturing for John to sit as well. This wasn't going to be standard, obviously. John wasn't a believer, or at least Mike was pretty sure he wasn't, so this was going to be heavy on the counseling and reassurance, light on prayer.

"So. What did you do?"

"I hurt Sandie."

Damnit, she had said she was being careful. Mike closed his eyes for a second, both worried and regretting that she was too far away for an I-told-you-so.

He took a deep breath and looked at the thing looking at him. "Okay. What exactly did you do that hurt Sandie?"

"I called Nacho."

Mike blinked, nonplussed, and John clarified. "On the telephone."

Mike shook his head. Of course the zombie alien couldn't narrate coherently. Of course. "And that hurt her? Wait, no, back up. What did you call him about?"

"Singing."

"More specifically?"

"Acquiring an agent, so I can sing for more people."

"It hurt her that you're trying to get an agent?"

"No."

Mike hung his head. "Oh, Good Lord."

It took a while and a lot of questioning, but Mike finally worked out that the issue was mostly the keeping of secrets. And of course doing something that he had known Sandie didn't want him to do.

"Have you apologized yet?" Mike asked.

John shook his head.

"Well, saying you're sorry is the best place to start. I honestly don't know what you could do to make it better. I mean, it's your career, so you can do what you want with it, but she does want what's best for you, so I can understand why she's mad that you didn't talk to her. So start with an apology, then ask what else you can do."

"I am not sorry."

"Yeah, I figured, but you can say it anyway. And you *are* here asking for my help, which means that you know you screwed up and you want to fix it, which is close enough to being sorry that it's not really a lie."

He squinted cautiously at John, trying to see something behind the hollow eyes and the mask-like face, something that would tell him he really was talking to a person who could care about Sandie and not a machine that cared only for so long as it needed her.

"You don't want her to feel bad, do you?"

"No."

"Okay, then. I think your heart's in the right place, at least. Now, you know that saying sorry and trying to fix it doesn't just automatically make people forgive you."

"I know."

"Good. Good. You know, I'm glad you came to me."

"You said I am not alone. You said even if no others come, I have you if I need you."

Mike smiled. "You do. And don't ever forget that."

He got up and retrieved two glasses of milk from the kitchen, one for himself and one for John. "Now, I am a little bit curious. More people is kind of what you need to get better, right? So why doesn't she want you to work toward that?"

John sipped his milk. "She is afraid of me," he said lightly. "She thinks I will take over the world."

Mike swallowed his milk a little too hard, and it hurt as it went down. "Oh."

=

John wasn't back when Sandie got up in the morning. She went to work, came home, and found three messages on her voicemail from Bert Gallegos, who didn't know that John didn't have his own number. She supposed she should eventually change her message so that it actually said her name, instead of just using the generic one that had come with the phone.

She didn't listen to the messages, either, just skipped through them with increasing irritation, not quite daring to erase them all, because that would just be mean.

There was one email from her mother, too, but it didn't actually have any text, so she deleted that. A second one came a while later.

Sandie, change of plans, we'll be home maybe in the summer to sell the house. We're living in Thailand now, you should come stay with us.

No asking how she was doing or anything. Sandie deleted that one, too, without replying.

It was nearly dark when Mike showed up with John in the passenger seat and dropped him off without staying to chat.

She and John stood and stared at each other for a while before she stood aside to let him in.

"I'm sorry," he said.

She lifted an eyebrow. "No, you're not."

"Mike said I'm close enough."

"I don't think you should do this. Not right now. Maybe later, but not yet."

"I know what you think. You're wrong. I will not hurt. I will heal, and I'll have money. You want money? I don't understand it, so you can have it. You're afraid because you don't understand me, but there are people..." He reached into her brain and pulled out the word. "There are scientists who understand things, and they want money, too. You can give them money to study me, and then you can understand and won't be afraid."

Aw, baby. Sandie sighed. It did make perfect sense. She did understand his reasoning. He wanted to be whole. And he was making such an effort, trying to be normal, holding a whole conversation with her out loud. But he didn't seem to be considering the cost.

"It's a really good plan," she conceded. "But John... you know what everyone is thinking, but you don't know the future, okay? You *are* different than you were, and you don't know how different you're going to get by the time this is done. I do want you to get better, but I want to go about that really, *really* carefully. Okay?"

He met her gaze steadily and nodded his understanding. "No."

TWENTY-SEVEN

Things started to roll ahead at an alarming rate, and John was suddenly inaccessible. She wasn't sure how he had become a functioning member of society overnight, but that seemed to be what had happened. He continued working evenings, and she continued driving him to work, but she had to cut him a house key and show him how to use it, because his days were taken up with the agent and various other professionals. He learned to use public transit.

Things were recorded, things were scheduled, things were hashed out and drafted and signed. It turned out that there were ways to work around the fact that John didn't legally exist. Probably not legal ways, possibly not even ethical ways, but there were ways. As long as someone was working on figuring out who he was and where he had come from, as long as someone was working on getting him a social security number, they all seemed willing to overlook the fact that he wasn't actually anybody just yet.

He was John Doe, a mystery, and they could capitalize on that. It wasn't really a gimmick if it was the truth. They built a persona for him, put him in futuristic suits with no lapels and reflective trim, and sketched a few rough posters showing a shadowed silhouette surrounded by multicolored laser beams.

THE SIREN, the posters all said in big letters across the bottom. Sandie guessed that if you didn't have an actual band, a weird stage name was the next best thing. At least it was an appropriate one. His voice was probably the closest thing to magic in the real world.

But they didn't talk. They almost never talked anymore, not even silently. She didn't try, and he didn't try, and the result was weeks and weeks of near silence.

She didn't even know there was a concert scheduled until a car showed up to take him to the college, where one of the auditoriums had been booked. Cheap college concert, of course – free admission to anyone with a student ID, five dollars to anyone without one – but it was bigger than anything he'd done yet, and he seemed as excited as he was capable of being.

He came back satisfied, because college students will go see anything if it's free and gives them an excuse to put that paper off a couple hours longer. And Bert Gallegos was thrilled, because they had just made an entire auditorium load of new fans. They would tell friends, who would go online to watch the preview videos they had posted, maybe buy a ticket to the next event.

It was boring. God, was it ever boring. Everything around Sandie was swirling like a hurricane, and she was stuck in the middle, in a little patch of nothing-much-going-on. Selling coffee every day had never been her ultimate goal, but it had been a lot easier when there were other things going on, things she could be part of. It had been easier when she needed the work to support someone other than herself. Now she had effectively booted herself out of everything interesting without actually managing to lower her stress levels at all. It was all still happening, but now it was out of her hands, and all she could do was watch.

John made small appearances and then bigger appearances. He kept himself going, and he healed. At night, he watched the darkness outside closely, waiting patiently for others.

"No others?" she asked him one evening, while his fingers moved over his guitar. There was paper in front of him, covered in sketchy musical notation. Somehow, she hadn't expected that he could possibly have bad handwriting, but it was awful, barely legible.

"I don't know," he said. "But if there are, maybe they didn't come because they didn't know where I am. So I'm calling for them, now."

Oh, good.

She made a point to ask questions about the proceedings, and though John rarely answered, he did let her know about the next big event, and she made arrangements to go to that one. The university again, free again, though this time, there were people in logo-printed shirts selling CDs by the doors. When the CD had come out, Sandie had no idea. She had asked, of course. John hadn't answered.

She sat near the front and was more than a little surprised – and more than a little disappointed – to find herself excluded, somehow. The music was beautiful, but she wasn't blown away by it, while everyone else seemed to be. She sat there uneasily as the people around her stared glassily forward, some swaying as though they might collapse, some with their mouths hanging open. What they were feeling was beautiful, she knew. It had never hurt her, and it wouldn't hurt them, but it was still frightening to see. They were entranced, and she wasn't, maybe because John wanted to show her that she personally had no reason to be worried about his weirdness. It sort of worked, and it sort of didn't.

The music, though... She hadn't put much thought into what his full-throttle singing would sound like to someone who wasn't touched by it, but she had figured it would sound like his work-mode singing. It didn't. Now that he was reaching for the big time, covering other artists' work and belting out classical and folk music wasn't going to cut it, and he had been writing his own tunes for a chunk of each evening. Now she realized that she had never seen him writing lyrics, because he wasn't using any. It was gorgeous, swooping, layered, like he was an entire choir wrapped up in one, but without any words. Maybe it was avant-garde. Maybe it was a problem. Maybe there was still something he could need her for; after all, she considered herself a poet.

She made a mental note to talk about it later.

There wasn't time, though. He was bundled off somewhere, and she wondered whether it was exactly as she had feared, that someone had identified greatness that couldn't take care of itself and was just using him. She hadn't pegged Bert Gallegos as the conniving sort, but she supposed any old jerk could fake a friendly smile.

There was a short-notice private event downtown at the Menger Hotel, somebody's birthday party, which probably wasn't very interesting after he had arrived.

There was something else in Kerrville, then an evening-in-the-park sort of thing, then another private party.

Then he just didn't come home at all, one evening, and Sandie had to call the cell phone Gallegos had given him.

"Where are you?" she asked.

"Austin," he said. "I'll be singing in an hour."

She didn't bother to fuss at him for not giving her a heads-up, just told him to be careful and to be quiet if he got home after midnight.

"No," he said. "Tonight, I'm staying here. I'll come back tomorrow."

Back, she noted, not *home.* It still wasn't his home, and it finally dawned on her that she sort of wanted it to be. Despite all her worries, despite the uncertainty, he had become a fixture, and she missed him now that he was always gone. The ultimate idea had always been to get him back to wherever he had come from, somehow, but now that thought hurt.

"Okay," she said. "See you then. Good luck."

She heard the phone hiss and crackle as his fingers brushed against it.

"Hey!" she called. "Hey!"

The crackling stopped, and she heard a breath against the microphone.

"I'm sorry, too, okay? I still want to help you with stuff, if you'll let me."

"Okay," he said. "But you are not an expert. These are experts, here. You wouldn't help. I'll see you tomorrow."

He hung up, and she sat down hard, grunting in

frustration. Then she made herself a bowl of ramen and went to bed.

=

The events got bigger. Maybe no one wanted her help, but by God, she could offer support until they all turned blue. She bothered John until even a creature that couldn't feel annoyance got fed up. He kept her updated on the schedule, at her insistence. Every little thing from his meetings to his recordings to his concerts.

And by that point, they were concerts.

It had been, what, three months since they had met Bert Gallegos? She wasn't entirely sure, what with John's life racing ahead and hers dragging, but it seemed both longer and shorter than that, and three months was about the middle point, so she went with it.

Three months, and John had been all over central Texas. He had a CD out and a YouTube channel and an official website and all kinds of social media accounts that he may or may not have fully understood.

And he was a big deal. The Herald described his rise as "meteoric," which seemed to be the default descriptor for nobodies who shot to fame overnight. It was also a pretty good descriptor for someone who may or may not have come from outer space, or from another dimension.

"What do I do?" Sandie asked Mike. "I don't know what to do."

Mike shrugged, "Pretty sure you're doing all you can. He's not *yours*, Sandie. He came to you for help, and now he's looking elsewhere for a different kind of help. Just because he's not human doesn't mean he doesn't have the right to steer his own life wherever he wants it to go."

"Unless everything goes wrong."

Mike smiled. "'Do not be anxious about anything, but in all things, by prayer and petition, with thanksgiving, present your requests to God.'"

"Does God care about aliens?"

"Not the point, baby. It means to do what you can, and not spazz about the things you can't affect. Do what you can, and for everything else, just let it go."

"Unless everything goes wrong."

He chuckled. "Pretty sure that counts as being anxious. Look, this guy's got a window into your head, right? He can see everything you think, ever. So he not only *knows* about your concerns, he *understands* them. And I don't know how much regard he has for the human race, but he wants *you* to be happy, and I don't think it has much to do with sucking the happy out of you. He cares about you. So I can tell you right now that he's listening, even if it doesn't look like he is. He won't hurt you if he can help it, and if taking over the world is something that would hurt you, *he won't do it*. See?"

"Maybe."

"Definitely."

"No, Mike. I'm not worried about him turning evil. Honestly, I don't think he actually understands good and evil. Hasn't eaten from the tree, or whatever."

Mike laughed. "Never ceases to amaze me when you show you've actually been listening."

Sandie silenced him with a glare. "What I mean is, evil isn't the problem. Ignorance is. I can't see him sucking the brainwaves out of the whole planet just for giggles, but I can see him making mistakes, hurting people without meaning to, or even hurting people while he's trying to help. He's like a horrifyingly powerful, terrifyingly smart *toddler*. And maybe if I was right there beside him, I could catch the mistakes before they happen, but he's not telling me anything, and so there's nothing I can do, even though it *is* something I could fix... He's letting me go to his concerts, but that's it. I'm not in on any of the decision-making."

She sighed and sipped at the milk he had gotten for her. "He doesn't have morals, Mike. He has logic. I've tried to talk to him a few times, but he keeps telling me that hurting people is *maladaptive*. Not *wrong*, but *maladaptive*. You don't destroy something you might need to use later. But if he ever decided that the human race wasn't going to serve a purpose later..."

She sighed again, harder and louder, so hard it hurt her throat. "I'd sort of like for him to be normal. Y'know, just a human being with some irregularities. I mean, what if *I* someday go on the no-longer-necessary list? I care about him. I care about him so much. But he doesn't care about me, he just needs me, and..."

Mike held her until the tears stopped and thought that maybe they shouldn't have gone through two six-packs of beer before hitting the milk.

=

The next concert was posh, a white-tie affair at the Majestic Theatre. As it turned out, it was actually pretty easy to book the Majestic, if you were booking it for a Thursday. Nobody ever did anything on Thursdays.

Sandie wore a sleeveless gown with a beaded bodice, a pumpkin-spice-colored thing she had bought for the prom she never attended, way back when. The saleswoman who sold it to her had said that it complemented her mocha skin and caramel-gold eyes, though mocha-pumpkin-caramel sounded to Sandie like a disgusting sugar overload, something a tourist from New York might order at the JoeHaus.

Mike was her plus-one in a tuxedo he had rather hilariously altered to accommodate a priestly collar, and Connie was *his* plus-one in a tuxedo with spider webs embroidered in iridescent thread, held together with safety pins.

They were a unique-looking group, and it was

entirely possible they wouldn't have been allowed entry if they hadn't been personal friends of the performing artist.

The Majestic was aptly named. Sandie had never been there before, and she thought it was the most beautiful thing she had ever seen in her life. All she knew of its history was that it had been built in 1929, and it was the definition of Jazz Age opulence. The theater itself was a Mediterranean street pulled straight from a rococo painting, its walls sculpted with windows and towers and balconies in an eye-boggling explosion of arabesques and flourishes in orange and blue and rust and gold. Candlelight flickered in the little fake windows, stars twinkled across the indigo-painted ceiling, and peacocks perched on the ornamented rails. White doves hung on wires, suspended in mid-flight. From her seat far blow, Sandie couldn't really tell whether the birds were fake or taxidermied. They were kind of unnecessary either way, she thought, but then, the entire magnificent setup was kind of unnecessary, and that was part of what made it amazing.

"Nobody could build something like this today," she whispered to Mike. "They couldn't possibly get away with it."

John was introduced. He sang. But there was something different, Sandie thought, something beyond the fact of her orange dress and the extravagance of the setting. It was a sort of turning point. This was the real deal. It wasn't Nacho's snazzy little dive or Mag's Bar or an auditorium full of bored college students. This wasn't a place for aspiring artists, but for the ones who had made it. John had gotten her and Connie and Mike in free, but it occurred to her suddenly that the men and women in the box seats, the ones whose glitter and shine hadn't come from a low-end department store, had *paid* to be there. Somewhere, they had heard about this miraculous talent that had to be experienced, and they had dressed up and shelled out. Not as much as they might have for other events, of course, but nothing that happened in places like the Majestic was truly cheap.

There was champagne afterwards. Actual champagne in actual glass glasses. There was mingling and cultured gushing among rich people who were so rich and so classy and so secure in their own affluence that they didn't even look down their noses at a woman in an old prom dress.

Somehow, John wasn't just John anymore. He was the Siren, and the Siren was a star.

TWENTY-EIGHT

The concert at the Majestic was the real deal, but it wasn't the big one, not yet. The big one took more months, and it took money, but money seemed to have stopped being a problem. The CD had taken off, the YouTube channel was buzzing, John was in the newspapers and all over the internet and on the sides of VIA busses, and he had to stop playing Mag's Bar and the Staghorn, because everywhere he went was crowded so far beyond capacity that the fire marshal made an appearance.

The big one was a slow build-up that started even before the hype exploded, back when it was still a gamble that had the potential to ruin Bert Gallegos and everyone who had agreed to back it, if things didn't pan out as planned.

The big one, as Nacho had promised that night in the

bar over a pitcher of beer, was the Alamodome.

Sandie had never been to the Majestic before, but virtually everyone in San Antonio had been to the Alamodome at least once, be it for a game or a convention or a band or the annual home and garden show, or just for somebody's graduation. In Sandie's experience, it took actual effort to avoid the place.

Still, she had spent years *trying* to avoid it, mostly because, like every other stadium on the planet, its parking was abysmally inadequate. There wasn't really any way to continue avoiding it and still show up and be supportive, so she climbed into Mike's van and let him try to finagle the parking lot. Mike consented, reluctantly. Connie offered to drive, but Connie drove like Mario Andretti on meth, and no one was interested in seeing how she fared against downtown traffic.

They parked, shuffled inside, and were ushered into the middle of a bustling hive of activity. Equipment jetted to and fro. Wires trailed across the floor like tentacles, attached to technicians in black t-shirts and baseball caps. Shouted instructions rang out, carrying too much jargon for anyone but a professional to make out the meaning. Sound checks rumbled and shrieked from inside the stadium.

They found John sitting quietly in a side room with Nacho and Bert. The agent paced, the beatnik sipped coke with his little finger in the air, and the musician fingered the frets of his guitar. John's suit had gone a step beyond shiny trim to full-on safety vest, a whole jacket and pants made of white reflector material with sparse green piping, which looked weird as he sat there but would probably look amazing under stage lights. He would glow.

"I've compared the numbers," he told Sandie softly. "I can't calculate something I can't quantify, but I think this should be enough."

Nacho and Bert glanced at one another in confusion, but she didn't explain it to them. They didn't need to know.

If anything unexpected happens, you'll stop, right?

no. unexpected is everything too broad not defined but I will not hurt.

Do you promise?

yes.

They sat in the middle of the organized chaos until it was time, and Nacho showed them to the super-special seats reserved just for them, right at the very front.

The stage had been set up at the far end of the stadium, and all the seats behind it had been cordoned off. That left three walls of tiered seating, plus the rows and rows of chairs that had been set up across what was usually the field. The backdrop was an accordion curtain of mirrored panels, and two monstrous screens flanked the stage, giving the unfortunate concert-goers at the very back a chance to see the Siren in detail. Not that anyone would be getting much use out of their eyes, not once it started.

The stadium filled. The lights fell. Clouds of smoke poured from somewhere behind the stage, lit from within by a dancing lattice of green lasers. The Siren stepped out from behind the curtain of mirrors. The lights found him, and he was suddenly blinding.

Sandie clapped and shouted and stamped with everyone else. His suit dazzled the cameras, turning both screens into blobby splashes of pure white, but from her seat at the front, just below him, she could see that he was right. It was going to be good. He hadn't even started yet, and the buzzing excitement all around was already buoying him up. His eyes were alive.

He held up one white hand, and silence fell like magic.

"Thank you," he said. Maybe there were microphones hidden somewhere, but Sandie didn't think so. His voice carried effortlessly to the very top of the stands without the distortion of electronic amplification.

And he began.

For a few bars, Sandie thought it was going to be more of the same, pure voice without words, but then the intro segued into a verse. Her lyrics, the ones she kept leaving beside his sheet music. Maybe she was excluded from the chemical spell he wove, but she grinned all the same.

When you fell out of the sky
and into my life
the heavens burned with nebula magic.
Blue stars in the dark
are the songs in your heart
you burned me, burned me with nebula magic.

Fire pours down
from the sun you sundered.
You fill me, beloved
with power, with thunder.

I set out to seek you, to touch you, to find you,
tame you and keep you, hold you and bind you,
not knowing the force of your nebula magic.
I thought I could touch you without feeling the fire.
Now the two of us, burning, rise higher
than the stars in your heart, your nebula magic.

It was corny. God, was it ever corny. He couldn't possibly have run it by any of his professionals first, or they'd never have let him bust out with her crappy poetry in public. But his professionals were all floored, enchanted. Everyone was except her. They all heard it, but she was the only one in any condition to listen. It was a gift between friends, a private moment in the middle of a crowd of thousands, a personal message. A promise not to outgrow her.

She shot him a quick thumbs-up. He didn't look, but she knew he saw. It was going to be okay. She sat back and let herself enjoy the concert.

He was rising, truly rising, expanding beyond the skin he had put on. She could feel that by the end of the first song. When she closed her eyes, she could almost see an outline, something that had been jagged and broken before, smoothing out and filling in gaps, making a new shape. By the end of the second song, she could feel it inside her brain and just under her skin, like tiny static shocks. Power. He was huge, far bigger than the man standing on the stage. But it was okay. That might have made her nervous, but she was keeping an eye on him, and he was letting her keep an eye on him, deliberately showing her that he was just healing, not turning into something unrecognizable. Five songs in, and there were blue and white lights in the smoke, flickering sparks of fire that Sandie didn't think had anything to do with lasers. There was a smell, too, something hot and sharp, like ozone, the smell of lightning storms, ionized air.

It was mesmerizing. He wasn't playing with the chemicals in her head, but she was very nearly lost in the spectacle, herself, when her cell phone vibrated in her pocket and jarred her awake.

Damn.

?

Nothing.

There was no reason to take the call. Whoever it was could leave a message, and she could call them back later. But she glanced to her right, at Mike and Connie and Nacho, then up at John on the stage. That right there was everyone who ever called her. So who...?

She pulled the phone out and glanced at the screen. International call.

Crap, crap, crap.

?

Nothing. I'm sorry, I'm just going outside for a few minutes. Promise I'll be right back. You're doing amazing.

She answered it while she dashed for the door, calling down the microphone as she did. "Hang on, it's really loud. Be with you in a second."

Shouting in the middle of a concert seemed unspeakably rude, but she didn't expect anyone to notice, and no one did.

"Sandie?"

"Mom?"

"Hey! Bet you're surprised to hear from me!"

Sandie pursed her lips. Damn, so this might take a while. The entire stadium was pulsing behind her, vibrating with a subsonic hum she felt in her bones more than heard. It was distracting. She moved out into the parking lot and toward Mike's van. "Extremely. Do you need something?"

=

For a long, long moment, the entire stadium seemed to hold its breath. Nothing moved, there was not a footstep, not the creak of a chair, not a shuffle or a whisper or a cough. Then a sigh went up from every throat at once, the tremulous release of the last of the energy that had built up.

Mike sighed as well and rubbed some of the goosebumps off his arms. Performance art wasn't really his strong point, but he thought it had gone well. It had to have helped, at any rate. Little bits at a time. And if it still wasn't enough, well, they would just have to deal with that. It sure looked like it had been enough, though.

Up on the stage, John raised one hand in a jaunty salute, the way he had been practicing. His face lit up the giant screen, and he grinned, huge and real, elated. The stadium ticked with a few scattered clusters of applause, those who weren't sure which was ruder: not clapping or breaking the awed silence. The sound gained a little momentum, died again, and then suddenly erupted in a thunder of stamping, screaming, whistling, and camera flashes. The air around John shimmered and undulated, either in the heat of the lights or with lingering vibrations.

To be honest, Mike hoped it was the latter, just

because that would be incredibly cool. It made for an awesome effect on the screen either way, one that the audience probably assumed was extremely expensive.

Amid the roar, John sauntered off the stage and across the field to duck out.

And it went wrong.

The camera followed him, so the entire audience had a clear view of the exact moment he stopped, hunched over as though in pain. A ripple, something like a shockwave, lashed through the air around him, and the microphones picked it up as a piercing squeal that gritted teeth and squeezed eyes shut everywhere as everyone simultaneously clapped hands to their ears. The entire stadium – the entire *city* – seemed to shoot sideways, like it had been bodyslammed by a fighter jet, from musical afterglow into panic. Blind, visceral fear that seemed to leach out of the stands, out of the ground, down from the sky. It was everywhere.

Someone screamed. Close by. Maybe Connie.

The parts of Mike that were still functional halfway expected a lethal stampede, a spooked citizenry charging for the exits and disregarding the human beings under their feet. Because he wanted to get out of there, too, but the sounds of mass exodus didn't come. A few feet pounded the stairs, a few bodies went tumbling, but everyone else seemed paralyzed, rooted to the spot, including Mike. He stood utterly, absolutely still, trying to run but unable, staring at the still form on the screen.

John shook himself and whipped around, staring down toward the place where Mike and Connie and Nacho sat. There was a message in that look, Mike thought, but it wasn't coming across very well. Then John pitched forward and ran. He disappeared through the archway and was gone.

Mike shook himself, too, and turned to grab Connie. She seemed dazed, gripping the arms of her chair with white-knuckled intensity, staring blankly at the now-blank screen as though it was swarming with eldritch horrors. He seized her arm, and she jumped, turning exactly the same look on him.

"Something's wrong," he said quietly, his voice shearing through the silence. It seemed like the understatement of the century. "Grab Nacho. We have to find John."

For a moment, he thought that he hadn't gotten through to her, but then she nodded. He understood. He had been able to get himself moving, but that didn't mean that he didn't still feel it in the pit of his gut, sharp, cold knives lurching around, trying to make him freeze solid like the rest of the audience. Well, he didn't have that luxury.

He got up and pelted down the side of the field as Connie turned to try to snap Nacho out of it. Down and down, through the eerie stillness.

The fear got stronger as he ran.

No, not stronger. *Louder*. Like running toward a blaring speaker. And when he paused to think about that – and to catch his breath – he realized that he knew where the speaker was. He could almost point to it. He could certainly go toward it.

Footsteps pounded after him, and he left Connie and Nacho to catch their breath, too, while he raced off again, burst through the glass doors, under the railroad tracks to the parking lot, and stopped.

John stood there by the curb, his body motionless, his head jerking around in tiny twitches with the force of his thoughts, like a bird trying desperately to understand something. Sound and emotion swirled around him like a riptide, fear and helpless confusion and pain. Mike could see it, or maybe it was just that the low, shattering frequency did something to his brain. Clear, lens-like ribbons of light floated like a cocoon around John, blurring his edges and distorting Mike's view.

But even through the bizarre distortion, it was obvious that there was something else there, at John's feet, and Mike's stomach clenched tight. There was really only one thing it could be.

"John?" he called. He stepped forward into the maelstrom. It pushed back against him with an actual, physical force, pounding against his skin as well as in his brain. He couldn't see a thing, and he realized that part of the problem was tears. "John?"

John didn't move.

Two clattering pairs of footsteps galloped up and stopped. Nacho's boots and Connie's heels. Mike held up a hand to keep them back.

"John? Can you rein it in? Let me through."

The storm abated, just a little, long enough for Mike to turn back to the others. "Connie, you got your phone? Good. Call an ambulance."

Connie fumbled wordlessly at her back pocket as Mike approached the scene.

It was Sandie, sure enough. The jagged black skid marks beside her said clearly what had happened. Her phone lay several feet away, smashed to pieces. Mike would have expected blood, but there was hardly any, only a few scratches, asphalt burns from where she had gone rolling and slid to a stop against the curb. There were no bones sticking out, no limbs splayed at weird angles. She just lay there, one arm by her side, the other draped over her stomach, her hair a mess, staring emptily at the sunshot sky.

There was no sign of the perpetrator. Nothing in the parking lot moved, not a car or a pedestrian or a pigeon. Hit and run, the miserable asshole.

Mike squatted down, reluctant to feel for a pulse. He knew she was dead, but he didn't want to *know* she was dead. Right now, he was safe. John freaking out behind him, the weird little noises Connie was making, Nacho's overly-loud breathing, that put him in the position of rational leader, and he could do that, at least until he *knew*. Knowing would open the floodgates, and then he wouldn't be useful anymore, and he had to be useful.

There was something else too, wasn't there? There was something he was supposed to be doing right now. Something *he* was supposed to be doing. It seemed glaringly obvious, but at the same time, it wouldn't come.

"Where did she go?"

Mike blinked at the question and looked up into John's white face, rippling and shifting behind the turbulent curtain of his own feelings. His own feelings. That was new, wasn't it? Probably noteworthy, but Mike didn't really care.

"Sorry, what?"

"She was here. She left. Where?"

Somehow, that was even worse than looking for a pulse and not finding one. She had gone, and John knew it, could feel it. The creature that had a link straight to her mind was looking for her, and she wasn't there. It was certain, then. Mike felt his face tighten and his throat close up.

"She didn't... She didn't go anywhere. She's just gone. I'm sorry, but she's just gone."

"No. It's damaged, so she went somewhere else. Where?"

"Heaven," Mike said numbly. "If I had to guess... She's... *was* a good person." Oh, right. That was what he was supposed to be doing. He crossed himself, began to kneel, realized he was already kneeling, and sighed.

"Absolve, we beseech Thee, O Lord, the soul of Thy servant Sandie, from every bond of sin, that being raised in the glory of the resurrection, she may be refreshed among the Saints and Elect. Through Christ our Lord. Amen."

But John was having none of it. "*No*," he snapped, his voice stiff and furious. "*Where is she?*"

It wasn't just grief, Mike realized. It wasn't just a horrified refusal to understand what had happened. It was a fundamental lack. John had no concept of death. He couldn't grasp the idea of a consciousness ceasing, leaving the universe entirely, going so far away it could never be found.

"Dead," he muttered, irrationally irritated. "She's dead, okay?"

He wasn't at all surprised by the stabbing pain that followed as a bit of the immortal bastard punched through his mind, grabbing at the word and the ideas that surrounded it. The creature picked apart the idea of death, scrutinized it, twisted it around and around inside

Mike's head, trying to find an angle that made sense. It got shredded, pieced back together, squished and molded and reshaped, then scrutinized again.

And again.

And again.

"She's dead," Mike repeated. "It's what we do. When we're damaged, we die."

Finally, the invasion stopped, and John stood still and silent, looking very small.

"They're going to take her away," Mike said gently. A breakdown threatened to tear him to pieces, but he held it back. Had to keep it together. He cleared his throat. "Going to take her body," he corrected himself, trying to speak so John would understand. "The doctors might try to fix her, but I don't think they will. If they do try, I don't think it will work." He wasn't a doctor, himself, to have a professional opinion, but he'd sure seen enough dead and dying people to have a good sense of which ones weren't going to wake up.

The shrill of an ambulance tickled the lower edges of his hearing, beneath the growl of I-37 and the weird, subsonic hum of John's turmoil. Maybe Sandie's ambulance. Maybe not.

"Fix her," John echoed in Mike's own voice. He made it into a question, but it wasn't. It was a promise. The writhing air around him stilled, ribbons of light withdrawing into his body. His skin glowed with the energy of it.

Mike understood. He wasn't sure how, but he understood, and he scrambled to get out of the way. He hadn't actually seen the zombie on Sandie's back porch, but she had described it to him, unmistakably dead, and now that thing was John, and John was very much alive, and infinitely more powerful than he had been then. What was dead had risen. It wasn't exactly a miracle, but Mike figured that if the Lord sometimes sent brilliant doctors to do His work, then maybe sometimes He sent aliens, too. Close enough.

He wasn't sure what to expect, though. Laying on of hands, or impromptu surgery... Even a song. John could do amazing things with sound, after all.

He didn't expect John to collapse where he stood in a boneless pile of polyester and white flesh, like a string-snipped marionette.

Connie shrieked and ran to him, propping the limp mass up against her side as she whispered to herself in Spanish. She peered into his eyes and scrabbled at his wrists. "I don't *think* he's dead," she muttered. "I don't think... There's a p-pulse, but..."

But Mike knew. "That's not him." He didn't want to get anyone's hopes up. He didn't want to suggest, even to himself, that it might be okay after all, thanks to the weird, incorporeal thing that had decided it wasn't

Sandie's time to go, so he didn't say anything else, only watched.

Nothing happened, not that he could see. Sandie's broken body didn't lift into the air in a swirl of sparkles, like it would have in a fairy tale. It didn't jerk around like it would have in a medical drama. It didn't melt and then re-form itself, space opera style. It just lay there, still and oddly rubber-looking, like it wasn't real at all.

But there was a tickle in Mike's bones, as of a sound either too low or too high for him to hear. The little scrapes and nicks slowly closed.

He bit hard into his tongue and waited.

And then she took a breath. Then another.

Sick with relief was a new feeling for Mike. He swallowed the bile that rose up and hung his head, muttering something he meant to be a prayer but that probably wasn't even words.

It was okay. Everything was okay.

Connie and Nacho seemed to realize what had happened simultaneously. Connie gasped. Nacho made a noise like a kicked dog.

John got back from wherever he had gone, and the body – with him back in it now – sat up. Connie squeezed him until his eyes bugged out, and Mike leaned over to grip his shoulder.

"You're a wonder," Mike said. "A saint."

"I fixed it," John said.

He wriggled out of Connie's grip and went to sit on the curb by Sandie's head.

"I fixed it," he repeated. "How long will it take her to get back?"

Mike froze. "What?"

TWENTY-NINE

The paramedics were bewildered. The doctors were bewildered. Everyone was bewildered except Mike, Connie, Nacho, and John, and they couldn't tell anyone what they knew. Maybe if they had known something that would have helped, they could have shared, but the bizarre knowledge they had wouldn't have brought her back.

There was money to keep the body going, keep food pushing down the tube in its throat, keep fluids dripping through the line in its arm, keep someone on hand to wash it and turn it so it wouldn't wind up with sores.

Someone, at some point, figured out how to contact her parents, and an email was dispatched. No reply came, and no one knew what else to try. Mike kept an eye on her email account, and Connie kept tabs on her home phone. They had to try to get in touch sooner or later.

John sat quietly in the ward until the nurses were in danger of realizing that he didn't sleep, and Mike finally convinced him to go home for a few hours.

Mike was lucky, in a way. Connie had a regular job that she had to go back to. No one was really sure what Nacho actually did for a living, but he apparently had to get back to that, too, albeit reluctantly. Mike had Monsignor Grigorio to take over his duties while he sat by Sandie's bedside and waited.

Maybe it would be okay. People sometimes recovered from being dead for a little while. It had been known to happen. But more often, they didn't, and though her heart was beating and her lungs were pumping, she didn't move. Her eyes didn't so much as twitch beneath closed lids.

He and John took turns. He waited, and then John waited, and then they waited together. Mike did his best to be unwaveringly patient.

John was less so. "How long?" he kept asking and kept asking, as though Mike's "There's no way to know" wasn't a valid answer.

Two days.

Three days.

A week.

No change.

"They don't usually just keep taking care of empty

bodies forever," Mike said candidly. "It's using resources that other people might need. Other people who will actually benefit. You need to prepare yourself. It might just be her time to die."

"Usually," John repeated. "Not usually, but sometimes?"

"Well, yeah, I guess. If you can pay for it."

"I have money. I can get more."

"I know you can. But if she's not coming back, it's not good for you to waste your time sitting and waiting for her. She wouldn't want you to."

"You are sitting and waiting for her, too."

Mike sighed. "Yeah. I guess I am."

And they waited.

Waited.

Waited.

The squeak of the nurse's walking shoes woke Mike. He watched her through half-closed eyes without a whole lot of real interest. It was the same old shtick. She came in, checked things, adjusted things, tweaked things, and left. He thought her name was Emily, or some such, but the truth was that he hadn't had the energy to pay attention to her name tag. Always the same nurse, though. That was dedication. Quiet efficiency and strength.

She didn't go to the bed, though. The squeaky walking shoes crossed to his chair, instead. He sat up abruptly, sure that something was wrong. Something had changed while he slept. Something had gone wrong, and he had failed to notice, failed to call for help...

Whatever was looking down at him through Nurse Emily's eyes, it wasn't Nurse Emily. It regarded him with cool, analytical, bottomless curiosity. It was enormous, incomprehensibly huge. He was a bug, it was a child, and between them, Nurse Emily was the magnifying glass. He leaned back instinctively.

"Others," Mike croaked. He cleared his throat. "Um, are you here for John?"

A picture forced its way to the front of his mind: John's smooth, bland face.

The thing analyzed that as well, and he felt its attention shift, zeroing in like a telescopic viewfinder on something across the room. Mike sat up and looked. John's body draped nervelessly over the arm of the other chair, empty. Its black eyes were already beginning to go dry and dull, and though it was still breathing, it wouldn't be for long.

"Oh," Mike mumbled. It was so surreal, he wasn't sure what to ask. He scrubbed at his eyes and looked up.

STILL HERE STILL HERE STILL HERE, said a billion voices in his head. *ALL MANY OTHERS NOT ALONE*

NOT ALONE NOT ALONE TOGETHER.

Two or three billion, maybe. One of them, in there somewhere, was John. Or it had been. The way they all spoke together like that, it was as though he had been absorbed.

YES. MANY TOGETHER ONE WHOLE ALL FEEL TOGETHER TOGETHER TOGETHER.

Another picture surfaced, Mike's own reflection zooming in and in and in to a microscopic level, thirty trillion cells making up one man.

"Oh. Okay. Good to know. Um... Where's the nurse?"

HERE QUIET QUIET TINY HEALER LISTENING HEALING LOST PIECE. QUIET QUIET UNDERNEATH WHILE KNOWING/SENSING/HEARING/UNDERSTAND-ING/TOGETHER-BEING.

"Did she say you could... use her?"

WE WOULD NOT HURT. ASK FIRST ALWAYS.

Mike rubbed tiredly at his stubbly jaw. Too much too fast, he almost thought, except that in reality, everything was going agonizingly slow. That was the price of heartache and sleep deprivation.

"You're going back to wherever you came from?"

There was a shimmer around the nurse's body, now, as though it couldn't quite contain whatever was in there.

YES.

"That's fair. I guess you waited long enough." It wasn't, though. It was horrible, and Mike crushed a spurt of anger. "If Sandie wakes up, I'll tell her you got what you were after."

The aura around the nurse flickered and sparked as cacophonous babble seared through Mike's head. It carried with it an undertone of distress. The organism thinking, he guessed. It had to be hell to think when every cell was allowed to have input.

FORGOT. FORGOT HOW? WOULD NOT FORGET. MORE US BIGGER EFFICIENT EFFECTIVE COMPUTATION PROBABILITY ATTEMPT...

The thought trailed off into babble again while Mike watched the nurse's skin begin to redden. A blister appeared on her lip.

"You guys should probably come to a decision and go. Wouldn't hurt, remember?"

WOULD NOT FORGET. FORGOT HOW? SMALL THINGS TINY ACTION MOVE WITH PRECISION...

The chattering thoughts ceased, and they went. The aura disappeared, and the nurse staggered backward, pressing her palms to her temples.

"What just happened?" she demanded.

Sandie sat up with a gasp and a stream of creative profanity that told Mike everything was going to be okay.

SEPTEMBER 20

Professionally known as the Siren, singer-songwriter John Doe passed away in the small hours of Monday morning, apparently of a heart attack, while sitting vigil at the hospital bedside of his best friend Sandra Melindrez. Amazingly and rather sadly, Ms. Melindrez, who had spent more than a week in an unexplained coma, had made a full recovery only hours earlier.

Mr. Doe's sudden and stunning rise to fame culminated last week in a final performance that attendees describe as "life-altering." His lamentably brief career produced a single album, "One Man Choir," as well as a number of popular singles including "Orion's Aria" and "Nebula Magic."

Little is known about Mr. Doe's personal life, but some reports suggest that he was a victim of amnesia and possibly suffered from numerous chronic illnesses, one of which may have been heart disease. Those who knew him decline to *comment.*

Mr. Doe will be laid to rest Friday afternoon at Post Oak Memorial Cemetery after services said at Our Lady of the Hills Catholic Church.

AD ASTRA

The money didn't run out. Sandie wasn't sure how, exactly, it had eventually reached her, whether John had inexplicably decided to write a will, or if it even would have been legal if he did, but some industry lawyer somewhere behind Bert Gallegos had taken pity on her. She was probably the closest thing John had to next of kin.

She didn't know where it came from or how legal it was, but she did know how to invest it, and so it didn't run out. It felt good to get the last signatures taken care of and know that now she had her own damn house that her parents couldn't just sell out from under her.

Same house, in fact.

And as it turned out, there were actually plenty of singers out there who couldn't write decent lyrics to save their lives. And public speakers who couldn't write speeches. And, amazingly, authors who couldn't write books. It was amazing, she discovered, what people would pay you to write things you wouldn't get credit for. Not a mind-blowing living, sure. She wasn't rolling in dough. But it came with more flexible hours than the JoeHaus did, which was good for someone finally finishing a college degree.

She learned to play the guitar. Not well, but well enough that she didn't look like an idiot when she took it to poetry slams.

She went out with Nacho once more, for old time's sake, and they both agreed that it should probably be the last time.

She wrote a memoir, then deleted the file, because no one would ever have believed it, and besides, she planned on writing a much longer, much more interesting one twenty or thirty or fifty years down the line.

And she was not at all surprised when, in the dead of night, a long, slight shadow fell across the frosted glass of her back door.

?

SUBSCRIBE TO M.R.
GRAHAM'S NEWSLETTER
AND BE THE FIRST TO
HEAR ABOUT NEW
RELEASES.

ABOUT THE AUTHOR

M.R. Graham is a native Texan who traces strong cultural roots back to Scotland, Poland, England, and Germany. A mild-mannered academic during the day, Graham transforms at night into a raging Holmesian loremaster and rabid novelist.

Though passionate about all scholarship and academia, Graham's training and true love lies with anthropology, particularly the archaeological branch.

Visit M.R. Graham at quiestinliteris.com or connect at facebook.com/authormrgraham.

Special thanks to my dear patrons,
and to Catherine and Maddie.

You can support the author and receive early access and special extras by contributing on Patreon at patreon.com/mrgraham.